Praise for Nancy Lindquist's
How To Conjure A Man

"HOW TO CONJURE A MAN is more of a comical romance than a sexy erotic story. There are a few hot sex scenes (like when Becky works the pole in the club like a pro when she thinks no one is watching) but the storyline is much more than a sex fest. ...Fun and funny, HOW TO CONJURE A MAN will have you smiling from beginning to end."

~ Ariel Summer, Romance Reviews Today

"Nancy Lindquist hits a home run with How to Conjure a Man. Between the electric chemistry flaring between main characters, Becky and Rick, and the sharp wit that kept me laughing throughout, this book is on my keeper shelf!"

~ Amanda Young, Author: Missing in Action

"Newcomer, Nancy Lindquist has penned a tale for Samhain Publishing that is original, funny, poignant, incredibly sensual and downright sexy. ...Can't wait to see what Nancy Lindquist does next!"

~ N.J. Walters

How To Conjure A Man

Nancy Lindquist

A SAMHAIN PUBLISHING, LTD. publication.

Samhain Publishing, Ltd.
512 Forest Lake Drive
Warner Robins, GA 31093
www.samhainpublishing.com

How To Conjure A Man
Print ISBN: 1-59998-404-0
Digital ISBN: 1-59998-242-0

Editing by Jewell Mason
Cover by Scott Carpenter

First Samhain Publishing, Ltd. electronic publication: December 2006
First Samhain Publishing, Ltd. print publication: March 2007

Dedication

This book has been a labor of my heart. A precious dream realized in a lifetime of untold blessings. I am forever grateful to my creator for allowing me this wondrous journey.

I'd like to thank my friend Becky. Not the Becky in the book, not anymore, but my friend is a delightful place to start. To Brenda, the sister of the heart. I love your soul. To the comma police, Mandi and my darling best-bud Amy. Love you two bunches and bunches. To my editor, Jewell. You make me believe in my writing. I can never thank you enough. To the Mistress of Purple, who always gets my jokes, no matter how lame.

To my friends who face and have faced the fight of their lives in breast cancer; Cash and Bunti, both cancer free for now and hopefully forever. Sue, who fights this demon every day...and to my dear, dear Serenity, who lost her battle two years ago and upon whom Vivian is modeled. Someday I will joyfully join you in the naked teapot ritual held daily at four in the Summerlands.

To my beloved Gene. If I could have conjured a man, you would be the one. Thank you for an amazing fourteen years and the most wonderful boys a mom could ask for.

Lastly to my mothers, birth and adopted. One for the gift she gave and one for the gift she cherished. Thank you for my life.

Chapter One

"Crap." Becky Blake wiggled her ass to the right. Nope, that didn't help either. The annoying, cactus-like object remained firmly wedged between her calves, prodding at her butt. Shoving her hand beneath her bottom, she raked the dry sand and grit of the desert floor in a blind search for the offending pokey-thing. Sightless fingers encountered what felt like a stick, *there*. In triumph she closed her fist around the object, yanked it free, and held it up to the moonlight. Ah, relief.

Huh, that definitely doesn't look like a stick.

Holding it to the light of what amounted to be ten pounds of candles, she struggled to put a name to the twisted stick-thing. She turned the warped, flattish item over in her hands, seeking any identifying hints. Finally, two empty eye sockets on one end clued her in. The nasty thing trying to poke her in the general area of her hind end was a dead dried-up snake. Slapping a hand over her mouth to suppress a scream, she tossed the nasty deceased reptile into the void of night.

Yuck, yuck, yuck. I want a shower.

Why on earth had she ever thought it would be a good idea to sit buck-ass naked out in the freezing cold desert? And for what? A man? She questioned her sanity for what felt like the millionth time. A quick glance at her watch only heightened the frustration that inched through her veins, eleven forty-three p.m. Exactly three minutes since the last time she'd checked it. Absently she rubbed her arms. The cold blue of the candles shifted to warm yellow and flickered off her goose-fleshed limbs. Midnight would never come.

Yep, she was having some fun now, oh boy.

She definitely needed a sanity check. Any minute now men in sterile white coats sporting nets would pop up from the austere desert floor and cart her off.

The muscles of her thighs burned from kneeling in the same position for the last twenty minutes on the chilly ground. She placed the instructions under her knee and wiped her sweaty, sand covered hands on the threadbare beach towel she'd found stashed in the trunk of her car.

Next time I've got to remember to bring a blanket. Ha! Like there's gonna be a next time.

Once more she looked down at her friend's neat handwriting, barely visible in the wobbly light, "How to Conjure a Man". That title had to be the lamest thing she'd ever read. She felt another poke in the rear and shifted uncomfortably. "Good Lord, what now? Isn't one dead snake enough?" Voice to the sky, she was not surprised when no answer was forthcoming.

Who the hell drives thirty miles out into the empty desert on a Thursday night to cast a spell for sex?

This was the damned dumbest idea in the history of damned dumb ideas. She'd spent an hour lighting the ninety-nine candles, placing them just so in the shape of a circle. Absently, she scratched at the itchy welts on her hands that marked the spots where melted wax had dripped on tender flesh. This whole experiment felt like a leap in logic equivalent to jumping the Grand Canyon on a tricycle.

As instructed, she'd tried to memorize the words her friend had so carefully crafted, yet they felt strange, almost like another language. They refused to flow out of her mouth in anything that sounded like human speech. Oh sure, they looked normal enough on paper, but when she tried to give voice to the ancient sounding poetry her tongue twisted over itself. Becoming frustrated time and again, she'd finally given up. Far better to just drag the paper along and read it as she cast.

Her best friend, Vivian, her partner in crime and resident strip mall witch, had sternly lectured that the flow of the words meant the difference between success and failure. Becky was going to screw this up, she just knew it. She always seemed to make a muck of anything that had to do with men. "In order for this spell to work it must be cast just after midnight on the day of the full moon." Vivian had repeated those instructions about thirty times. She'd claimed it had something to do with birth energy, and while Becky had assured her friend she was not interested in birth of any kind for a few years, at least, she was going to follow those instructions to the letter. Yep, she was pretty desperate.

She was seriously in need of a man. Her vibrator just did not cut it anymore. Not one little bit. In fact, the stupid thing had actually stopped working the other night mid-fantasy. She should have brought it with her to bury along with the list of requirements for the perfect male specimen she'd carefully written in the special ink. It would serve it right for pooping out just when she needed the purple monster the most.

That's loyalty for you.

She'd shown it years of devotion and love. How dare it die in her time of need?

Stupid thing.

She'd almost bought a new one she'd seen in a catalog. Labeled as a massager, there was only thing you could massage with a device that small. It was flexible, had various attachments and the price had been right. Instead, she'd poured her heart out in a long session of tea and sympathy to her friend, Vivian. Now Becky lived the end result of that conversation.

Somewhere in the distance a coyote howled.

Cripes, that was scary.

In a well lit campground, with her friends all around, the sound would have been lonely, almost romantic...but alone, right now, in the darkened desert? Maybe not so much. Another quick glance at her watch told her it was almost time to cast this puppy.

Becky's thighs ached now. Gravel, dirt and assorted pointy objects dug into the tender skin of her knees. She glanced down at her thighs. Their lengths glistened smooth and clean under the rays of the full moon.

Apparently Viv thought a trip to the local spa and a full Brazilian wax made for better conjuring. Either that, or she took pleasure in torturing Becky for no apparent reason. As soon as the hair started growing back she was going to itch big-time. Her eyes roved over her newly oiled and denuded body, stopping at the point between her breasts where the light flickered against a simple silver heart locket. Filled with herbs, the locket would be the focus of the night's work. It was to be charged with the intent of the spell, worn until she found her man. The thin metal gave her the illusion of being almost clothed. Her only other adornment, a watch, did not.

Carefully, Becky opened a bottle of scented massage oil Viv had mixed just for this working. She placed it with care on the rose colored cloth she'd laid out in front of her. Near enough for anointing, but far enough away to be safe from her shaking hands. She rocked back on her heels and surveyed the scene. Her mind whirled as she looked into the circle from her vantage point outside the northern edge. She mentally checked off the list of items she'd gathered for the ritual and placed on the altar she'd erected in the middle of the circle earlier. Dagger, oil, incense, all in place. Once more she caressed the locket, bringing it to her lips. Did she have everything set out like she'd been instructed? Doubt filled her. She bent her head to read the words Viv guaranteed would bring her the man of her dreams.

Damn. It's hard to see out here.

Her torso tilted as she bent forward to catch the light of the candle denoting north, which left her teetering dangerously close to the flame. Anxious to better make out the neat yet small characters on the paper, she tried to focus her eyes in the dim light.

Howwwl.

"Holy. Fucking. Shit." Her body jerked and her eyes shot wide open. That coyote was close, too close. Her gaze narrowed to better search the darkness on the other side of the ring, more than half expecting to see the furry creature. Nothing. Still wary, her attention was drawn to a strange glow that emanated from near her right hand and the paper she gripped. One edge turned orange, then blue, as fire licked in an almost slow motion march across the surface then flashed into a ball of flame. Shock contorted her features as Becky saw the entire purpose of tonight's exercise disappear before her horrified gaze. Too distressed to even try to put out the miniature inferno, she held it tight until the heat became too much against the sensitive skin of her fingers. Dropping what was left of the spell to the ground, she watched as the parchment pulled into itself. It writhed into a tight, useless, blackened ball on the bare earth.

She snorted. Well this was a fine kettle of fish. Hours of preparation, tons of work and the perfect—according to Vivian—time of the month, wasted. Just gone in a moment. Now what? Glaring out in the general direction of the howl she shook her fist in the air. "You think you're cute don't you? You know, I have no problems with coyote fur hats! Right now I'm pissed the hell off, so you'd better watch it buster."

Fabulous. Telling off the local wildlife had to be yet another sign she was certifiable.

As she saw it she had two choices. Pack up all this stuff and head home, trying it again next month, if she had the nerve, or do as much as she managed to remember and hope and pray she got it right. Not that she expected much. Vivian had full faith in the magic she created, and her belief spilled into every part of Vivian's life.

Becky didn't quite share her friend's level of faith.

Crud, she might as well just give it a go. She was already here and it had taken her so long to put this together. Getting her nerve up for this one attempt had been hard enough. She doubted there would be a second time, not without copious amounts of wine, and Viv had told her not to drink before trying magic. Viv, oh no, what would she tell her friend? Vivian had spent so much time researching this spell, fine tuning it for Becky. How could she tell her friend she'd gone to all this work for nothing? Becky felt like three hundred kinds of a fool. *But, nothing ventured, nothing gained.* It was time to decide. She could step into the glowing circle or she could run away afraid of her own shadow. What was that saying? There's no bigger fool than the person who does everything the same way and yet expects a different result. She was dead tired of the same result.

What's it going to be, Beckers? Is tonight the night you try the path less traveled or do you crawl back under your rock?

"Screw it. Circle the wagons, boys, Becky Blake's going in after her man." Her voice sounded lonely and small in the thin desert air. Sighing in resignation, she gingerly stepped into the middle of the circle of glowing orbs. Each one added an eerie air to the already mysterious night as their light pooled in the surrounding dirt. Moving to the center she lay down as Viv had instructed, head to the north, arms pointing to the east and west, legs spread. Hopefully nothing was going to crawl where nothing should crawl. A giggle escaped her lips and she slapped her hand over her mouth fast. This was supposed to be a serious endeavor.

How the hell am I supposed to be serious splayed out like this?

What were those instructions? Oh yeah, first she was supposed to blank her mind. *Easier said than done.* In the silent baking heat of the day, death was everywhere. At night the desert became a living thing, full of sound and energy. The silken evening opened seductively to become a poet's playground. Reaching for the ritual knife she'd borrowed from her friend, she placed it over her lower abdomen. The slightly warmer skin retreating from the cold metal sent ripples over her tummy.

She opened the rose scented oil and touched it to the places she'd been instructed. Pubes, below her belly button, stomach, between her breasts, throat, forehead and the top of her head. The sweet-scented oil felt warm and tingly against her cool bare skin, almost erotic after the chill of the metal knife. Stretching her arms out once again in the positions dictated, she took a deep breath and prepared to call to the forces of nature. She could not remember the words. *Think Becky, think.* She had to remember the damn words. Cripes, she couldn't. She knew they rhymed, but beyond that, what? Drat, she was gonna blow this big time. Yes, part of her felt stupid, yet a

13

bigger part hoped with all her heart that Vivian really could help find someone that met Becky on all levels. She wasn't getting any younger here.

She was supposed to mentally call to her dream lover, exemplifying his characteristics without describing any one particular man. Easy enough, she could do this, she really could. She'd read that parchment a thousand times. She could totally wing it. An odd mix of confidence and fear filled her belly, cascaded over her body. It flowed from her stomach and down to her toes, and then up to the top of her head, filling her with energy and purpose. She pulled in one, then two deep breaths. She felt calmer, cleansed. The breaths removed all but her purpose from her mind. She crossed her fingers and began to speak.

"Aphrodite, Goddess of love, she whose beauty fills the heavens above. Bring me a wonder, a man among men, someone to love and lust after time and again." Not exactly perfect, she reflected, but it didn't suck either. Okay, maybe she could do this after all.

"Make him handsome, with a full head of hair, yet not his whole body, except for down there." She giggled. This was sort of like going to a burger joint and ordering a man.

I'll have a number three with a side of beefcake and large penis, please.

"Bless him with muscles, hard to my touch, and give him a large penis, but please not too much. Fill him with lust only for me. I'm not interested in someone who's randy, you see. Make him smart, not so much he's an ass. A sense of humor is good, but please not too crass."

Okay, she was getting into this now. In her head a form began to take shape, she could almost see the outline of a powerful masculine body before her. Wow, this was amazing. She should have tried this years ago.

She continued, "Please make him sweet, roses and poems. Oh and make sure his friends are not all gnomes. Fill him with purpose, a desire to please, and in the bedroom adventure to..." Damn, she was stuck. What should she say about his performance in the sack? "...and in the bedroom adventure to striptease?" Oh good grief, not that, she got enough of that at work. This was bad. She would just have to start again with the sex part.

"...and in the bedroom sexual adventure to please." Well she'd used "please" a whole lot, but hopefully Aphrodite would not have an issue with it.

"Dear Aphrodite, all this I ask, in the face of your love, for causes so vast. That my heart and mind might be full of desire and his also and may never the fire, be banked from our hearts, our heads or our loins. That together we two might one day soon join."

Now, how did that last part go? Viv had said that part was the most important of all. Frustrated, she wracked her brain. Oh yeah, now she remembered, or close enough she hoped. "Three times three I call thee. Three times three I charge thee. Three times three I bind this sacred spell to me. As I will it, so mote it be." Her voice rose almost to a shout as she finished the spell. The air around her, previously alive with sound, became silent and still, as if something beyond her voice held the breath of the hungry animals foraging in the night.

The sky, which had been clear while she waited to do this bit of drama, emitted a distant sound of thunder...not unheard of in a desert that rarely yielded rain. A greenish blue light flashed behind her closed lids and her eyes flew open in alarm. She sat up, the hair on her arms standing to full attention.

What felt like hot breath hit her ear and she jumped with a shout. Looking quickly to her right, she stared into the candlelit expanse. Was there someone there? Something beyond the light? Nervously, she lifted a candle from the protective circle and held it high. She sighed in relief, laughing at her vivid imagination. No one was there. Just vacuous dark and the same cactus that had been her companion since she began this idiotic misadventure.

Pack it up, kid, and head home. This place has gotten inside your head.

As instructed, she lifted each candle in turn and blew a gentle breath over the flames, releasing each one with thanks until she was left with only north, the representation of herself. She grabbed her flashlight, flicking on its feeble glow while she puffed out the last small fire. The yellow circle cast by the electric torch felt impersonal and cold compared to the warm light that had surrounded the space moments ago.

As she reached for her robe, the coyote let loose another baleful mourning cry to the silver radiant moon. She shivered uncontrollably, quickly gathered her things, and stuffed them haphazardly into her bag. After digging a small hole with a new shovel, she dropped her list of qualities for her conjured dream stud into its depths with an ironic little lift of her eyebrow, then covered it over. Time for home and coffee.

Chapter Two

Screw coffee. Time to haul out the big guns. Hot showers fix almost everything, and right now she was in desperate need of a de-stressing. She'd stupidly decided to come up the Strip on her way home, something she normally never did, but it was so late and a weekday to boot. How darn busy could it be? She'd been willing to chance it. As the crow flew, it was the most direct way home. Too bad there was a convention in town. The bleeping, blaring horns and the obnoxious smell of exhaust in the chilly night air made her feel claustrophobic after the solitude she'd enjoyed in the barren wilderness. Living near Las Vegas Boulevard made it easy for Becky to get to the club, which was just off that adult wonderland, but it was a pain in the damn ass to go anywhere else in a car.

She'd sat in traffic for almost an hour, and now it was two in the morning on her only night off this week. She'd already wasted enough of her time in foolish pursuits for one evening. After all that, getting stuck in traffic had been almost too much. She pulled her spiffy red convertible into the parking spot in front of her condo, rested her head on the steering wheel for a moment, and enjoyed the feel of relative solitude and quiet of the parking lot.

She loved it here in Las Vegas, the pace of it, the feel, the weather. Most of her friends couldn't believe she'd left a promising career as the head of a large accounting department in Chicago to run an all-male strip review in the Mecca of sin. Their skepticism and teasing remarks had shown Becky that none of them had truly understood her heart. Besides, she would have done anything for her crazy grandma Lucy.

The woman was the best part of Becky's life. When the old lady had retired to Italy with one of the club's strippers, she'd turned the whole thing over to Becky. Lock, stock, barrel and all fifty hunks of hot, man-meat strippers. Becky hadn't been able to resist the siren's call to a new life. The truth was, she'd been dead bored in Chicago. Nothing exciting ever happened to her and the winters could be brutal. Lucy was Becky's only remaining relative and she loved her madly. It had taken less than a minute to decide to jump ship, sell her fortieth floor condo on Lake Michigan and head west to her new life.

Her grandmother's dear friend, Vivian, had immediately taken Becky under her wing. Happily, Viv provided her with dinners, listened to her woes and made it her number one priority to stick her nose into Becky's love life on a regular basis. The brash redhead was nothing if not meddlesome as hell. Becky felt right at home under her tutelage.

Gathering her thoughts as well as the bag of miscellaneous crud to take into the condo, Becky climbed out of her car. Even in the dead of night her community was alive with people coming and going. Not as busy as it would be in a few hours when the sun rose, but people still dotted the lot. They headed to cars, hauled in groceries, chattered together, even at this hour. It felt good to be home.

Door open, the smell of newness and home surrounded her in welcome. She'd bought her condo sight unseen off the developer's website, a risk that had made her almost physically

18

ill. The building boom in Las Vegas meant that you had to move quickly when you saw something you liked. She'd been lucky, this condo was perfect for her. Two bedrooms, two baths and a view overlooking the pool from the third floor, it was exactly what she'd always pictured her home would be one day. Sleek with marble kitchens and baths, plush cream carpet and warmly painted eggshell walls. Touches of her soul she'd gladly paid extra for. By the time she'd finished tinkering with the space, the sale of her old place in Chicago and the purchase of this condo ended up to be an almost an even trade, yet worlds apart in looks and feel.

Entering her comfortable bedroom filled with warm cherry wood furniture and cream and gold art always made her smile. The bed, covered in a light down comforter complete with brown and cream duvet, had been a pricey purchase. But it had been worth it. The warm snuggliness of her haven meant everything to her.

Shucking the red sundress she'd been wearing for her foray into the wilds of the Nevada desert, she headed into her bathroom. She couldn't wait to get the desert dirt out of her hair. Scratchy skin, covered in a fine layer of dust, begged to be clean again. Besides, she needed to wash off whatever germs had covered the dead snake. Shuddering, she turned the taps and climbed in.

The hot water fell in a heavenly rush over her weary body. It slid down over grit-covered skin in a luscious flow. Sandalwood soap, one of Vivian's creations, slipped over her, filling the air with heady warm scent. Closing her eyes in the simple pleasure of warm water, she turned her thoughts, once again, to the night's activities.

Would it work, this plan of Vivian's? Her friend had sworn the spell had brought her George, her husband of forty years, but Viv also believed dancing around naked under a full moon

19

was what made her shop so successful. The more practical Becky figured it had more to do with the lucky amulets "The Moon's Daughter Occult Shop" sold to the gamblers who lived in or visited their fair city.

Turning off the shower with reluctance, Becky stepped out and covered herself with a fluffy towel. She needed to get some sleep. It was almost six a.m. The first interview for a new bartender was less than eight hours away. Why did Tad have to quit now? Okay, so he was getting married and planned to move to California, good reasons, she admitted with a rueful smile. Still, she hated to lose him. He'd been at the Buckin' Bronco for years and had been a huge help when Becky was in over her head as the new owner—a condition that still occurred far too frequently for her tastes. She'd received a stack of applications for the job, though, and winnowing them down had been easier than she'd thought it would be, yet still tough.

Weeding out anyone without actual bartending experience had left about twelve potential Tad replacements. Whoever she picked had to start soon. It would take most of the head bartender's remaining days to teach the new guy the ins and outs of selling drinks to a bunch of horny women hell bent on having an amazing night out.

Sitting at the vanity in her bedroom, she gathered her mass of long chestnut brown hair in her hands, pulled the soaked mass over her shoulder, and began to detangle the length from the bottom up with a wide tooth comb. Long and pin-straight, it was her greatest conceit and her greatest nuisance. She'd thought about cutting it many times, but memories of her sweet mother running a brush through it always stopped her from taking more than an inch or so off the ends. Her mom had loved her hair, and keeping it long helped Becky hold her memories close.

The comb pulled painfully at the knots, jerking her mind away from the past and into the sleep-fogged present. A deft twist of her hands resulted in a long braid flung over her shoulder to hang midway down her back. Braided, her hair would dry in her sleep giving it the waves it naturally lacked. She pumped moisturizer into her hands and smoothed it over one tan leg, then the other as she massaged away some of the stress held tight in her muscles. The creamy white lotion was essential here in the west.

The changes life had wrought in her soul over the last six months seemed to show visibly on every part of her body. She'd lost weight since the move. Tight small muscles now delineated along arms and legs where they had never been before. Stress, a sunny climate to work out in and odd hours had changed her, inside and out. Now she wanted a man, needed, she amended. She had to face facts here, she was lonely.

The first flush of learning the ropes at the Buckin' Bronco over, she was busy, yet not so busy she didn't have time for love. At the core of her heart, Becky was a romantic. She believed in true love, and in all the fairy tales her mother once read to her at tuck-in time every night. Not that she wanted a hero to rescue her. She didn't need a man to wall her into some modern day ivory tower. Just a soul-mate to share her stress with, her joys and hot sex. *Just a soul-mate.* She laughed. It was a tall order, this hope of hers. Her eyes wandered to the trashcan which entombed the carcass of her bright purple vibrator. That was no longer a satisfying option.

She wanted love and human to human sex. Not just any love or any sex, but lasting love and damn hot sex. Stuff that she'd only read about in the erotic romance novels she parked herself on the treadmill with, lurid covers and all. Sure, she got some odd looks, but they didn't bother her. The books made the time fly.

Slipping between the cool clean sheets with a happy little sigh, she closed her eyes. The nights work in the desert receded, pulled away like a commuter train leaving the station. Yawning, she turned over into her favorite sleep position, willing her body to give into the dream that scampered around the edges of her foggy brain.

Chapter Three

Blinking, Becky sat up and gazed around her in confusion. She seemed to be back in the circle in the desert. How did she get there? The candles, all lit once again, glowed blue, carnelian and alabaster around her. Eerie flashes of color leapt over her bare skin. Standing, she paced the circle north to south, then to the north again as she completed the circuit. As she passed each candle, its flame soared skyward, growing up around her until the light reached just over her head. A wall of flame enveloped the space she stood within. Like being in the eye of a hurricane, she could still see black sky and stars above her, the moon hanging over all.

The wall of flame filled her eyes. It pulled her step by tentative step, against all logical thought, into its fiery depths. Her heart pounded as she drew close to the eerie wall of patterned light. She moved a tentative hand to within an inch of the dazzling liquid fire. A prickling sensation shot energy through her and tingled over her body and out her feet to the earth beneath her.

Curious, she pushed her hand further. This time it passed it through the wall of fire. It felt cool to the touch, yet it spread electricity through her in a sizzling haze. The electric energy snapped around her, almost lifting her from the ground. Light without heat sparkled through her body in waves of arching fire needles. Jerking her hand back she inspected it closely. It looked perfectly normal to her, unscathed. Placing it back into the flame's wall, she began to walk around the circle, left hand outstretched into the barrier of light and color. Moving clockwise faster and faster, now running, joy filled her heart, seeming to flow from her in palpable waves. The intense release of energy danced from her, glowing brightly behind her as she circled the ring again and again.

Starting to spin in a tight twist she twirled, a whirling dervish under the bright full moon—her audience of one— hanging in the sky. Laughter filled her belly, rippled to her lungs, pushed against her vocal chords, then broke free in a primal shout. Dizzy, Becky fell to the ground breathless, her chest heaving up and down, the lines of her body a perfect mimicry of before. Head to the north, arms outstretched, legs splayed. She was waiting...for what? Her arms seemed to grow into the ground, becoming one with the soil. Palms down, she stroked and petted the dry dust, reveling in its velvet texture.

Did the stars see her as they twinkled so close above? A sexual sacrifice placed upon an altar of burning need. A precious gift laid upon an ancient slab awaiting the monster. Would he devour or love her?

Desire filled her and the need for sexual release swarmed in her veins. Buzzed through her like hornets surrounding a nest. Reaching her hands to her neck she began to caress her body, slowly traveling down over her sensitized shoulders. Tingles trailed after her fingertips as she teased her nerve endings into shivering want. Her hands moved lower, momentarily cupping each of her breasts, pinching the hard sensitive nipples. One hand wandered lower still to caress her waiting pussy. An eager finger entered her slit. Slick juice covered it in liquid satin. She moved it up to brush over her clit which sat like a ripe little berry on top of a parfait, waiting to be plucked and tasted.

Was that a noise? Strangely, the fear that had driven her from the ring of candles earlier in the night was not there now. Almost leisurely she sat up, staring with sexual hunger at the large red candle that marked South in the sacred space.

Shifting and shimmering, the colors moved, the fiery curtain drawing back upon itself, as if parting for a performance. Squinting her eyes, she peered beyond into the inky black desert night. Padding restlessly at the edge of the candlelight was the largest coyote she'd ever seen. Presumably the one she'd heard when the parchment burned earlier in the night, but there was no way to know for sure. Reason seemed far away, ungraspable.

The animal's great muzzle rose high as it smelled the surrounding air. Mid-sniff, the massive head stopped, then turned in her direction, its gaze leveled on her naked body. A myriad of colors washed over its face in the shifting candlelight. Rough shaggy fur covered its body. Immense paws flowed into spindle thin legs which in turn supported the powerful torso.

Snout lowered, the creature advanced towards her, one wary step tracking another. She knew she should be afraid, she was pretty sure that fear was the appropriate emotion when one had the world's largest coyote heading for your naked ass. She waited, no fear came. Wariness, she felt plenty of that, maybe even a trace of anticipation, but no fear.

Reaching the edge of the now split curtain of fire, the relentless movement of the furred body halted. Becky's eyes widened in astonishment as the light seemed to arch out, wrapping around the coyote, moving over him like a living thing, running fingers through the rough fur. A shaft of pale moonlight beamed over the beast, then joined with the fluid color to lift the great animal into the air. Whisper soft illumination balled around the helpless animal, all grace and flowing light.

25

As she watched, the creature became taller, broad of shoulder, furred limbs becoming devoid of hair. Its body rolled in the fire-filled light, tumbling upon itself. Paws molded to form hands, and the long muzzle shortened to be absorbed into a human face. Spindle thin legs filled out, became muscular, flowing into slim hips. The now wide, brawny chest tapered to a slight, smooth waist. A thin line of hair ran from just below his belly button to the patch between his thighs, which only highlighted the thick erect penis thrusting proudly between them. Finally, the fire traced hot blue light from the top of his head down over the strong muscles of his back, replacing itself with silken hair, the rich hue black volcanic sand against naked tan flesh.

Her eyes feasted on the gorgeous body floating in the flaming orb at the edge of her circle. Powerful and sexy, the desire to run her hands over the suspended perfection proved too much. Curious, she rose and reached out a tentative finger to touch the sphere of light surrounding the glorious male inside. It sparkled, then drew her hand in with a crackling snap. The air all around smelled of electric, ozone and sexual desire. The wall of his muscled chest stopped the forward progress of her questing fingers as light arched in a brilliant, sky-filling display, then winked out. The thump of his feet hitting the earth reverberated through the ground beneath her. He stood before her in a semi-crouch, his posture wary.

His face in filtered shadow, half covered by the fall of ink black hair, she couldn't quite see his features. They shimmered, out of focus, as if the fire of transformation had not wholly finished its work there. She noted a white feather twined in his tresses, the alabaster spine of it gleaming against the rich hue of his silky hair.

He stood, his body rising to its full amazing height before her astonished gaze. Her breath came in hot puffs, the sight of him filling her with wild anticipation. She dropped her head and squeezed her eyes closed hard. This sex God had to be an apparition; men did not from coyotes come. She peeked one eye open to glimpse the ground. Nope, his rather large bare feet, the color of baked earth, still appeared as if formed from the desert floor. Dang, right here, in her circle, within touching distance, was the hottest, sexiest man Becky had ever laid eyes on in her life.

Thank you, Aphrodite.

He appeared to assess her with a feral sniff. A hand reached out to stroke her hair with almost gentlemanly kindness. The soft touch belied the erotic need she felt pulsing from his body. He held back, like he was afraid she was not quite real. She almost smiled. This man was way out of her league and yet she felt his wanting hunger for her, saw it in the hard cock jutting between them. Raising her head, she licked her suddenly dry lips. Against the skin of her thigh she felt his cock twitch lustily. The movement quieted the beat of her heart. She was almost afraid to breathe for fear that any slight movement would cause him to fly away, dematerializing as magically as he'd appeared. The last thing she wanted was for this man to disappear.

His hand moved through her hair in a slow mesmerizing journey. Whisper soft, it traveled to her jaw where a strong thumb pressed over her lips and seemed to revel in their texture. The thumb, exuding tender pressure on her mouth, pulled her lips apart and slipped slowly into the moist cavern. It moved between her teeth, stroked her tongue. She licked over its surface. He tasted of earth, salt and warmth.

Joined by his other hand, he held her face captive still stroking in and out of her wet mouth. Sexual desire filled her to overflowing. Eyes closed, she relished the feel of his thumb flicking over her lips and tongue, agitating her body to heated need. A hand tingled over her skin to her collarbone, then rested against the hollow, the fingers playing with a strand of her hair. His thumb pulled tenderly from her mouth. She sighed. With the sweet assault over, she felt a little lost, missed the feel of him inside her. Fingers traveled down her arm to brush the side of her breast and stopped there, as if he sought to gauge her reaction.

The touch tingled through her, shot between her legs to form a pool of erotic warmth in the damp at the apex of her thighs. His palm slid with almost tortuous slowness over her nipple, lightly caressing the puckered pink flesh. Thumb circling the nub, he gently pinched the dusky flesh. She felt hot and open and willing. Needed him to continue with the sexy story that raged against her common sense. Any lingering fear melted into white hot lust and combusted in a hiss of desire.

The heat that had been absent from the light before seemed to fill her now, centering between her legs to radiate out in every vein and artery. The moist folds of her sex creamed with the touch of his hands on her. She sucked in her breath, her tummy rippling with the effort to breathe. Hard fingers clamped over the tender skin of her nipple drawing a startled gasp from her lips. Half closed eyes shot open to search the absent features before her. Her flesh sizzled under his touch. Dropping her head back she pressed her curves against him. It felt so good to be touched by his rough fingers. She wanted everything he could give her, the very cells of her body cried for the promise of release his hands possessed.

Becky's hands began to roam over the hard planes of his body. At first tentative—a feathered touch to the powerful neck, fingernails against his shoulder. Emboldened by the strangeness of this encounter, she moved lower, over the defined abdomen to the indentation where a powerful leg met his torso. He was beautiful, a statue of living bronze in the

28

aurora of light. Defined muscle, sleek under satin skin, covered his chest. Lightly she teased him with her fingertips. His sharp indrawn breath spurred her on, made her want him to beg for more. Boldly her hands wandered over him, no hesitation, no fear, no wondering if she was doing the right thing. Only a deep need to feel this magic man's body beneath her fingers.

He moved his hand to her other breast to repeat the same action, alternately caressing then abrading the sensitive nipple. This time, lips parted, a cry erupted from her throat, raw with lust-filled need. The sound pleaded with him to fill her body with this strange ghost man born of desert and her desire.

He must have understood the wish borne in her transparent gaze. Abruptly, he lifted her against him. The length of her legs wrapped the strong column of his torso. His cock rested over her pussy, making sweet promises of the dangerous pleasure to come. Dropping to his knees he laid her body down with almost tender affection on the soft earth. His bulk loomed over her large and powerful. Air forced from his lungs moved in ragged gasps against her cheek. His hair covered her face in an onyx curtain, glossy and thick, shielding them from any glowing eyes prying in the night. It gave her a feeling of warm safety, erasing the last of her inhibitions. She looked up, needing to see into his eyes. His face shifted in the light, yet would not come into focus.

His hand cupped her face, stroking it softly. She felt possession in his touch, but no ownership, only mutual mind searing pleasure. The rough hand against her soft skin moved to her neck, sending shivers over her body. His erection pressed hard and urgent against her thigh. If possible larger than before. She moved her leg against it, rewarded when it jerked in need. His upper body lifted off hers, held aloft by straining muscle, allowing her hand to touch the soft skin that covered the rock hard member. A fingertip flicked over the bead of slick wetness at the tip of his engorged cock. She pulled in a shuddering breath, then moved the finger to her mouth to suck the taste of him into her. Salty, with an indefinable sweetness that made her want more. She felt his hungry eyes travel over her mouth, search over her body in a blatant caress. An aroma of musky need emanated from him, singeing the nerve endings wherever his body touched hers. His face moved lower, closer, a breath alone separating the space between them and still she could not make out his features.

An animal-like growl issued from his throat as lips and tongue replaced the hand on her neck, the heat searing her flesh, branding it. Sparkling energy surged over her as she arched her back, pressing herself against the hard massive length of his body. His thigh rested between her legs and she pushed into it, rubbing her pussy against his thick muscles.

His hand slipped down to her flanks as he shifted his leg, replacing the hard thigh. His fingers brushed her labia, then expertly circled her clit, dipped shallowly into her slit, then slipped out again. He toyed with her, never staying on her button for long before moving away, his touches light, almost teasing. Her hips followed his fingers in wordless need, desperate for more, seeking the release his fingers promised. His hand stilled and sharp teeth tenderly bit into the flesh of her neck. *Message received* she thought and pushed her bottom back to the dirt, forcing herself to remain still, allowing him to orchestrate their erotic dance.

Her nails raked lightly down his back, and hard muscles bunched beneath her fingertips. Breathless, she waited for his next move. The thick length of his cock pressed insistently against her thigh, moved erotically over her skin. He groaned against the sensitive shell of her ear, almost too soft to hear.

Gentle fingers returned to her clit. They moved faster now, shifted from her wet slit to the hard bundle of nerves. Fourth of

July sparklers danced through her body. She focused tightly on the sensation, blocked all other thought from her mind as she concentrated on the awareness he sent through her body. *Feel, just feel,* she urged her mind. A shout ripped from her body while her toes curled helplessly. Her head flew back. She stared at the starry sky above, her body shattering in orgasm. Her face buried in his neck and shoulder while he held her tight to his hard warmth in a soothing embrace.

Panting, the world swam into sharp relief once more. She wanted to taste him. Fill her brain with the musk-covered, sexy scent of his balls while she sucked him to ecstasy. She licked her lips, imagining his cock throbbing and powerful, his thick cum shooting down her throat. She reached for him, pushed his shoulders until he lay on the ground beneath her. It was his turn now and she couldn't wait to get her mouth on him. Her hand reached out, caressed the long hard shaft sensuously. She smiled at the quiver of his flat stomach, then kissed the spot beneath his belly button where the tip of his cock glistened with pre-cum. The flat of her tongue darted out and licked over the sensitive flesh she found there. She rolled her tongue over him to savor the salty taste of him. The skin on her hand where she held the base of his cock began to tingle. One moment his body was hard desire beneath hers then he was gone...flashing white television static where flesh had been mere moments before. Fleetingly, he appeared solid under her once more and then the world winked out.

⅜ ⅛

Becky gasped. She was covered with sweat, sitting up in her own bed, her own room, her own home. Damn, only a dream. Her hand rested between her thighs, fingers covered in slick cream. A sad, lost feeling filled her as she stared at her hand. She felt almost guilty for pleasuring herself, something she had never wasted that emotion on before. She'd wanted him to be real. Too bad the sexy man who'd touched her so intimately in the sacred circle had been no more than an erotic fantasy. Turning to her right, she glanced at the time. Ten minutes to eight. Normally she slept until noon. She tried going back to sleep, rolled over more times than she could count. No matter what she did, her body thrummed with sexual need, telling her no more sleep would come this day. Fine with her, she had interviews to prepare for anyway.

She tossed her legs over the edge of the bed and wiggled her cold toes in a sunbeam that snuck around a crack in her blinds. A flutter in the radiant light caught her eye, and the movement startled her to stillness. Her eyes caught the lazy motion of a feather as it danced slowly down toward her in the morning ray. The white outline of it haloed in light as it drifted to rest between her still damp thighs. Wonderingly, she picked it up. What the hell? It must have hitched a ride from the desert with her, still... It looked so much like the one that had been tied in her dream lover's hair.

Her laughter filled the silent room with sound, breaking the tension that filled her. Her thoughts flitted fancifully through her head. Dreams didn't reality make. That whole spell thing had put her imagination into overdrive.

Better get up, nut-ball, time to go pick out a new bartender.

She opened her nightstand drawer to put the feather away. Placing it inside, she began to push the drawer closed, then hesitated. She wasn't ready to put her sexy dream lover in a dark, cold corner, yet. Humming a happy tune, she picked the feather back up, then headed to the coffee maker to begin her day.

Chapter Four

Something yanked at Rick Frazier's brain and dragged him mentally kicking and screaming from the beautiful woman he'd been making love to. It jerked his mind cruelly awake despite his determination to remain in a rock-hard-cock dreamland. He couldn't place the irritating noise, it ate at his ears unceasingly.

"Please, shut the fuck up."

The polite "please" apparently worked. Blessedly, the exasperating noise stopped. *Relief.* Rolling over, he scratched his balls and melted into a yawn, willing his mind back into the fire-lit circle.

Shit, there it was again.

Whatever annoying pain-in-the-ass with the nerve to call him before nine was about to get an earful. Okay, maybe not an earful, but he was definitely annoyed. Everyone that had his number knew he worked all night and slept late. Everyone that had his number respected his need for rest. Everyone except... Crap, it was Tara.

Eyes shut tight, he reached toward the annoying phone, blindly banging his hand over the top of the coffee table. Tonight he'd make sure he left that sucker on vibrate. Checking the display he groaned. A large letter X to denote her position in his life glowed up at him. What did she want this time?

Pasting enough of a smile on his face so as not to sound pissed when he spoke, he smashed the talk button. "Good morning, Tara."

"Good morning, Rick. Is this a bad time?"

Yes, you know darn well it's a bad time, that's why you're calling me now. "Why no, it's a great time. I'm always up this early.

He didn't want to cheese her off. She always went into full drama mode when she sensed he was pissed. Rick felt too tired to be on the receiving end of one of her rants. He rolled his neck around. It felt sore from yet another night of crashing on the couch. One of these days he was gonna learn to crawl into bed before he dropped exhausted where he sat. Cupping the back of his neck with his free hand, he massaged the aching muscles while he wrestled with the monumental task of keeping his mood as mild as possible. Tara always seemed to know what buttons to push. That trait had made their sex very good. Too bad the rest of the time he felt like an animated marionette.

"Oh dear, I think I woke you up. Gee Rick, I'm so very sorry." Her bored tone told him she was nothing of the sort. "Listen, now that you're awake, I need to talk to you."

"Okay, fine. Can we make this fast though, Tara? I have to get some coding done, then I have a job interview." Oh crap, he hadn't meant to say that out loud. Rising, he began to pace around his coffee table.

"Really?" He could almost hear the cash register dinging in her brain. "That's fabulous. Something corporate, I hope?"

"Umm, not exactly," he hedged. "Just a bartending gig."

"Oh, is that all? Geez, Rick, why are you even wasting your time with crap like that? Didn't you get that out of your system in college? You'll never amount to anything slapping drinks around in a bar."

His throat felt dry and tight. "Maybe I have to take a job because at the moment I have limited assets, Tara. You don't happen to know why that might be, do you?" Damn, why did she have to call before he was awake? He didn't want to fight with her. He just wanted her happy, not with him, but happy nonetheless.

"Rick, when are you going to let that go? He screwed me too, you know. It wasn't just you who got it up the ass. Right now he's sitting on a beach somewhere with all my money and some sizzling chick in a bikini bringing him drinks."

"No Tara, that's where you're wrong. My ex business partner is sitting on a beach somewhere with all *my* money. You just stole it from me via the court system then passed it on to him."

"Shit, Rick, you're so damn bitter. I thought we moved beyond all that. Look I have a problem and I need to talk to you."

"Is it about money, Tara?" The silence on the other end told him he'd hit the nail on the head.

"Well, sort of," she admitted.

"Then you're talking to the wrong person. There's a guy on an island somewhere you can contact. I have to get some work done before my interview." He moved the phone from his ear in preparation to end the call. A thin pleading on the other end stopped him.

"Rick, wait. I'm really stuck here this time. Can't you just help me out one last time?" She was begging. He imagined her face right now. It would be all helpless kitten eyes and pouting lips. He'd fallen for this act so many times before. Could see the drama unfold with his eyes closed. Tara held a black belt in using sex as a weapon.

"Except it's never the last time, Tara." Damn, he was being too harsh. He didn't want to hurt her. They had been through enough pain already. Softening his voice he continued, "Why don't you go back to your parents, Tara? They'd love to help you out. Just call them. I know they miss you. Don't cut them out because of your pride."

The sigh on the other end sounded exasperated and a little sad. "I will. I'm just not ready yet, Rick. I feel like I let them down so badly."

Irritation crept back into his voice, "You let me down too, Tara, and you have no problems calling me." It felt like he was preaching to someone not the least bit interested in conversion. No amount of talking on his part was going to change her. He knew that, so why did he even bother?

"You're different, you're my Rick. You'll always save me. I don't know why you won't give us another chance. It was only one teensy mistake."

"Not to me, Tara. I will never trust you again. Fool me once..."

"I think you're being unfair, but I won't push you. You know I never push."

"Uh huh. So what's the real reason for this call?" Was this woman serious? How could she actually spew this garbage without laughing?"

"I need to borrow some money. I'm about to be evicted."

Pulling the phone away from his ear, he stared at it. He could not believe what he was hearing. "Evicted? Tara, I sent you rent money two weeks ago. What happened?"

"Well I have all these interviews and I need to look good for them..."

"Are you telling me you spent the rent money on clothes?" Looking up, he took in his bare walls, lack of furniture and the basic comforts that made an apartment home. He'd left her with almost everything, wanting no reminders of the pain she'd inflicted. He'd learned to live on less, much less, why couldn't she?

"I have to look like I can fit into the corporate world. It's been so long since I held a job. Please, Rick, I really am trying here."

He could hear her crying now, the soft sobs muffled by the phone and distance. The next stage usually involved guilt, then she'd morph straight into yelling. He could just give her the money and get her off his back, or put up with many more phone calls just like this one. Running his fingers over his scalp, he yanked his hair back, hard, and sighed.

"Okay, Tara, I'll send you some money."

"Oh, Rick, thank you." Her voice turned bright and cheery, a rainbow after a hailstorm. "Thank you so much. I'll look for the check. Toodles." No long goodbyes, not real appreciation. Typical Tara.

The line went dead. All he had to do now was write out a small slip of paper with what amounted to his remaining savings in dollars and cents and kiss it goodbye. He stared at the phone for a long time, half expecting a tiny fairy to fly out of the receiver and tattoo the word, "sucker" on his forehead. He'd gone from giving in to Tara's demands to make his life peaceful in their shared space, to doing it to make his life peaceful hundreds of miles away from her. Oh yeah, he'd progressed since the divorce all right.

She was making a pussy out of him and he was damn tired of it. It was long past time to nip this whipping in the bud. A long phone call to her family would probably fix things once and for all. It was time to move her along and get her out of his life for good. She may bring annoying clinginess to a new level, but the fault was not hers alone. No one had forced him to give in to her demands over and over again, and by doing so he had helped create his own Frankenstein's monster. Instead of cadavers, this one was made of cash and designer shoes.

When his former partner cleaned out the joint bank account he'd shared with Tara, Rick felt sorry for her. Poor Tara had never been good at making her own way in the world. Always a princess in an ivory tower, she expected men to save her. It was easy to play hero to her helpless doe-eyed demands. She'd fully expected Rick to bail her out, and he'd been all too happy to jump head first into the role of hero, cape flapping in the wind of his own self important fart. He should have cut her off at the knees when he'd found her sucking his former partner's dick.

You have a lock on stupid sometimes, Frazier.

Running a hand over his jaw, he banged the cell phone down on the coffee table harder than he needed to. He should be more careful, he couldn't afford to buy new electronic gadgets right now. His lovely ex-wife was busy bleeding him dry. Money was tight.

He headed into the kitchen and dropped a pod into his coffee maker. A cup of Joe would bring perspective.

Oh how the mighty had fallen.

Owning a software business had led him to believe he'd never have to make coffee for himself again, unless it suited him.

Whine much?

Taking a swallow of the glorious life-affirming liquid he practically lived on these days, he tried to mentally put his discussion with Tara into a neat file, lock it up and concentrate on the day ahead. It was going to be interesting, no doubt. What the hell did you wear to an interview at a strip club? Maybe a robe with nothing under it 'cept what yer momma gave ya. That would be appropriate. He chuckled. The lady who'd set up the interview told him it was casual, jeans would be fine. He'd not worn them much since college. He looked forward to being comfortable while he worked again.

The corporate computer world meant suits for meetings and sweats for the days he sat hunched over the gray box banging out code. Now that his business was gone, run into the ground by his vindictive former partner and now ex wife, he needed a change of wardrobe. Welcomed it.

Five years of his life had been flushed down the drain in a combination of bad asset management and legal fees. Served him right for trusting anyone other than himself with the books. When the business folded he'd worked tirelessly to make it as right as possible, finishing computer programs without pay. A few of his clients had reimbursed him for his time anyway, managing to keep him afloat, barely. Others had sued him and his now absent partner. It had taken everything Rick owned to pay off those debts, but he'd done it, and was proud of it. What could have been the ruin of his career was only a setback. Reputation intact, he had clients lined up and ready to go. All that was left was a final tweak of the software he'd finished a couple weeks ago. It was damn close to being saleable. He only needed to get by a little longer, make the rent for a few more weeks. This bartending gig would make the difference between a great product and one rushed to market before it was ready.

He yawned. He was exhausted and yet he had to be sharp for this interview. As he sipped at the hot coffee, his thoughts floated back to the dream. Rick was a normal man with normal needs. Hell he'd been having highly charged sexual dreams since he'd been about thirteen. Still, he could almost smell the

39

heated skin of the woman he'd driven to orgasm with his fingers. The damn thing had felt so real. He'd wanted to bury his throbbing cock in her sweet, tight pussy and fuck her till she screamed his name.

He remembered the feel of her. The hot need in her eyes as he touched her pretty pink moistness, sliding in and out of her with his fingers while she panted and writhed beneath him. The cold of the desert was palpable until her heat in the circle of fire seared him.

Her body, so ripe and luscious, had responded like a warm gift beneath his. She'd reached for him, pulled him to her with sexy promises in her pretty brown eyes...until the damned phone had started ringing, jarring him out of his fevered state.

Damn, that had been some dream. He was hard again just thinking about it. "Down boy, we have an interview to get through. Then I'll buy you a new tube of lube." He snorted. Yeah, this was the life. His cock's sex partner now was Rosy Palm. He remembered all the jokes his friends used to tell about going blind from playing with yourself too much. Good thing that was an old myth. If his penis didn't like the new state of affairs, too bad. For now, flesh and blood women were off the menu. He loved sex. Still, another knife in the back was something he was pretty sure he wouldn't be able to survive. It'd taken him too long to heal from the last one.

Who the hell did he think he was fooling? The wound was still fresh. Only a thin scab covered raw flesh. He didn't love Tara anymore, but there was a lot of regret there. Regret for all the dreams that died the day he'd found her sucking the person he'd thought was his best friend's cock. He wished she'd just move on with her life and stop calling him all the damn time. He was tired of her manipulative bullshit, just about at the end of his rope with it.

He shook his head. Time to shift focus. How casual was this interview? Could he get away with a clean T-shirt? Rooting through his closet he pulled out his "Property of the Cheyenne Nation" tee, and tossed it on his bed. Might as well answer any questions about his ancestry right away. Besides, it was the most comfortable thing he owned.

A hot shower revived his tired mind. Toweling the fog from the mirror, he ran a brush through his long straight hair, then pulled it into a neat ponytail, securing it with an elastic band. A pair of jeans joined the T-shirt, completing his interview look.

He stepped back to survey himself in the silvered glass one more time. It wasn't a suit and tie, but then again the hair had never really gone with the suits anyway. He was as ready as he was gonna be for this interview.

Grabbing his wallet off the desk in the corner, his fingers brushed over a sheaf of papers, knocking the top bill off the neat pile that awaited his attention. Reaching down to retrieve it, his eyes scanned the considerable back due amount highlighted in vivid yellow. He never thought he'd be working for someone else ever again, but life had taught him to expect the unexpected. Until he sold the program, bartending seemed like a good way to stay ahead of the shut-off notices. This job would be easy enough, if the sultry voiced woman he'd spoken with on the phone hired him at all. His skills were rusty at best.

Thinking about the voice of the owner of the Buckin' Bronco All Male Review reminded him once more of the dream he'd had last night. He'd bet anything that the bar owner, Becky Blake, had nothing on the hot angel he'd happily pleasured while he'd slept. Good thing, cause that was one complication he did not need.

Chapter Five

Out came the red pen for the twelfth time today. Writing a big "no" over the face of the application, Becky placed it in the growing reject pile. Another one down the tubes. Too bad the guy had been all looks and no brain cells, she thought. None of these applicants would work at all as a potential replacement for her lead bartender. One had clearly made up his previous experience. He hadn't known a Cosmo from a draft beer. The one thing a bartender at the Buckin' Bronco needed to be familiar with was how to make "fru-fru" drinks.

The second guy was more interested in tossing his hair around and flexing his biceps than the actual work. Call her old fashioned, but Becky still believed questions about lunch hours and perks of the job should not be the first things a potential employee brought up the moment they sat down.

Candidate number three was the worst of the lot. Somewhere along the line he had confused "male strip club" with "house of prostitution", making it crystal clear that he was more than willing to service the clientele. He hadn't been seated five minutes before he'd offered Becky cunnilingus on the floor.

Ick

Numbers four through eight were either badly out of shape or had a frightening amount of back hair. Becky hated turning down anyone based on appearance. It wasn't fair, yet their clientele had certain standards in strippers and bartenders. Becky's goal was to offer her ladies the ultimate male dream come true, men so hot they sizzled. Back hair, and paunch did not spell sex to most of her patrons.

The last guy had the most promise, that is until he started asking questions about dating the rest of the staff. Becky had no issues with hiring anyone who was gay, several of her strippers were. She just asked them to be careful not to let on to the ladies who paid big bucks for their fantasies. This guy had let her know, in no uncertain terms, that he was here to meet men. While dating among the staff was not prohibited, he struck her as too aggressive, making her think he was going to spend more time chasing tail than pouring drinks.

She dropped her head to her hands. This was a mess. Along with the three no shows, that left one lonely application left, Rick Frazier. Since he wasn't due for another half hour she had time for a much-needed break. Standing, she stretched her cramped limbs. Her bottom ached from being plastered to a chair for the last few hours. Still tired from her adventures the night before, she headed around behind the sleek oak bar and poured herself a Virgin Mary, dropping in a celery stalk and a dill pickle.

Mmm, lunch.

"Well, how the hell did it go?"

"Hey, Viv, have a seat. Can I pour you a drink?" Becky nodded indicating the stool across from her. The brash Occult shop owner looked particularly interesting today in a bright orange skirt and flowered summer hat. Viv always dressed like a ten-year-old's idea of a psychotic gypsy. Colorful skirts, turbans or hats in exotic materials and enough banging clanging jewelry for fifteen regular people. The shirts she wore were the only sedate things about her. They were always a somber black to contrast with the vivid red of her hair.

Late at night, when she was cleaning the bar, Becky sometimes made a mental game of playing, "what color is Viv's hair in real life?" She was fairly confident no one had that answer, not even Viv.

"Sure as shit, hon. Gimme one of those fancy waters you charge through the butt for. Then tell me how the spell went. I'm dying to know."

Becky was not going to get out of this conversation, not that she thought she could. Viv had a way of yanking secrets from her that set her teeth on edge, but there was never any malice in the older woman's heart. She loved Becky. With her family gone, Viv made a heck of a substitute.

"Oh you know, I went, I saw, I cast." She smiled, poured a glass of chilled Pellegrino and handed it across the bar.

Viv accepted the offering with narrowed eyes and took a long sip. "You know that's not even going to come close to cutting it right? I want some serious dirt."

"Okay, I'd love to. Can we make it speedy, though? I have another dumb-ass coming to interview for the bartender position in a bit."

Vivian winced. "Ouch, hon, that was harsh. Your day been that bad?"

Becky ran her hands around her neck massaging her own sore muscles. "You're right, Viv. That was just bitchy. I'm sorry, but you should have seen the guys I've met with today. Most of them either have no experience at all, or plenty of experience, but something was off. Oh and then there was the guy who wanted to have me interview him between my thighs. I tried to tell him there was no legal prostitution in Las Vegas, he didn't get it. I've got to replace Tad soon if we're going to make this transition seamless."

Her friend chuckled. "There's your problem, Beckers, your expectations are too high. No transition can ever be seamless, dearie." She took another long sip of her water and then stared at the glass. "Never did know why people think this stuff is so much better than what comes out of the tap, except the tap stuff's not fizzy. How much does this cost those suckers you call customers?"

"Four fifty." Becky grinned. "They're happy to pay it too. All the other clubs in town have a cover charge and high drink prices. We just rob 'em with four dollar water."

"Hmm, I'm not sure I'm enjoying this enough then." Viv took a longer sip, appearing to roll the water around on her tongue. "Nope, it's still water." She set the glass down on the bar with a flair of her hand. "So how hard do I have to beat you to get information out of you? I'm not going to ask again."

Becky grew serious. "You know I don't buy into everything you sell over there, right?"

Vivian nodded in agreement. "Just because you don't believe in the magic, hon, does not mean it doesn't believe in you."

"I wasn't expecting anything to happen, not really, but I'm so damn lonely, Viv." Becky didn't feel at all odd telling this woman the truth, raw and painful as it was. There was something about Vivian that coaxed honesty from her. As far as Becky knew, Vivian never so much as told a white lie in her life. She was goodness and sincerity personified. Being less than truthful with her would have been a slap in the other woman's face.

"I went out there, into the desert with your stuff—which, before I forget, is all in my trunk—and I did what you told me to, all of it. Right up to the part where I was ready to cast the actual spell."

"I sense a, 'but' coming on, what happened?"

"I burned it," she mumbled.

"Oh dear goddess, you what?" Viv's skin began to match her hair color, starting at her neck and working its way north.

"I didn't mean to, Viv. I leaned near a candle to read the parchment and it went poof."

"Poof?" Her voice definitely sounded a bit strangled, something was up.

Becky nodded. "Yep, poof."

"Becky, this is important, did you say the exact words on the paper?"

Becky shook her head. "Nope, I tried to memorize them, but I couldn't. I know I got most of them right, but not all."

"Why didn't you use the flashlight I sent along?" she asked, a curious tone in her voice.

Becky's brows knit. "You mean you can use the flashlight during the spell? Won't that make for bad Juju or something?"

Viv shook her head, vivid red curls bouncing and bobbing with every wobble. "Where do you mundanes get this stuff? 'Bewitched?' Spells are about intent, honey. Burning that spell and casting a hit or miss version was not the best thing you could have done, Beckers." Shaking her head one more time, she stared into space for a heartbeat then looked back at Becky. "Shit, well you better hope I worded that thing well, that's all I can say."

"Why?"

The redhead drew in a deep breath. "Because burning is just another way of putting your intent into the cosmos, calling your needs and desires to you. There are many ways to cast a spell child. Burning words on paper, speaking them, releasing a vile of charged fluid into water. The means are almost as endless as the people who send out the energy. Normally, a witch would pick one of these methods, if the spell had strong intent, perhaps two, but that can have the effect of placing a sort of double whammy on the magic. The call could be very strong at that point. You want to unleash the desires of your heart, not be caught in a hurricane of wish fulfillment. So, what happened after you cast?"

Becky felt herself heat from the top of her head down. "Umm, well I cast the spell and went home and went to sleep. Then I woke up and came into work."

The painted on arch of Viv's eyebrow rose with long practiced ease. That was some eyebrow, Becky thought. Without saying a word, Vivian could use it to coax entire deep dark hidden secrets from the most reluctant of the people she performed readings for. Vivian's raised brow was a work of expressive art, conveying a range of emotions and thoughts with a mere movement of muscle. Becky was helpless in its raised glory.

Rats.

"Well I sort of had an erotic dream." The other woman stared her down. "Okay, not just any erotic dream, but— steaming hot, I could smell his skin on mine, had an orgasm in my sleep—erotic dream. Other than that, there isn't much to report."

Reaching down behind the bar, she began to re-arrange bottles, the ones she had just spent yesterday afternoon straightening up. Anything to hide from her friends all-seeing eyes.

Viv chuckled delightedly. "Well that's great. Sounds like you met the man you called in your dreams, Miss Becky Blake. That's fabulous. Congratulations, dearie."

Becky's head popped back up over the bar fast. "Oh no you don't, Vivian McDonald. Don't you go attributing my naughty dream to your spell. It was just a dream, probably a coincidence. I haven't had sex in so long my body was desperate. Nothing magical in that."

"Think what you like, dearie. I know a magical tale when I hear it. You need to look at this more closely. There's no such thing as coincidence in this world. It's all what we send out and are receptive to," she intoned knowingly. "The question now is, are you going to allow the magic in, Becky Blake?"

The sparkling green of Vivian's gaze bored into Becky's. She had the feeling her friend could seek out all the dark places of Becky's soul, laying them bare to the world if she wanted to. With anyone else, Becky would have walled herself off, but she trusted the priestess.

Viv continued, "I can't bring you the love you need, hon. I wish I could. Maybe, just maybe, our energy together can open the door for the person who can." Reaching her big body over the bar with surprising grace, she placed a kiss on Becky's forehead, stroking her hair like her mother once had. The gesture brought a tear to Becky's eye.

"I'm glad you're my friend, Viv. Thank you for the spell."

Her friend's eyebrow lifted in that amazing arch once again. "Don't you mean, 'thank you for the spell, even though I am pretty sure I wasted a cold naked night in the desert for nothing'? Cause I'm pretty sure that's what you meant."

Becky laughed. "Quit reading my mind, you old witch."

"Well then don't leave it wide open for me to tiptoe through, young lady."

She hefted her substantial body off the stool and headed to the exit, loudly singing, "Ding Dong the Witch is Dead" from *The Wizard of Oz.*

Becky laughed as she piled the two used glasses next to the few she had to wash before she opened the place at eight.

Might as well get them done now.

She filled the three sinks in front of her with warm water, the prescribed levels of soap and clean smelling bleach. Humming the song Viv had sung, she began to clean the glasses.

The hot rush of dry Nevada air wafted into the club, bringing a smile to her face. Not bothering to look up from her chore, she called as the person pushed through the swinging, saloon-style doors just past the main entrance. "Came back to dig at me some more with your hocus-pocus, witchy woman?"

"No, I'm looking for Rebecca Blake."

The voice washed over her like liquid heat and smooth velvet. It stroked her flushed skin in an aural caress that flowed over her so unexpectedly she felt physically touched. Her hands, buried almost to the elbow in the bleach water, stilled as her eyes lifted to the man who filled the doorway.

The glass door of the main entrance behind him flooded the foyer with daylight, simultaneously haloing the man's outline, yet not allowing her to focus on his features. He was tall, tall enough so that she would have to look up if they stood next to one another. His body formed a perfect V shape, broad shoulders melting down to a trim waist. He shifted restlessly, waking her from her stare session and spurring her to action.

Heading around the bar, too late she remembered to grab a towel for her wet hands. Shrugging, she wiped them down the front of her jean-clad legs, leaving long damp trails behind.

Holding a mostly dry hand before her, she pasted on a nervous smile. "Hi, I'm Becky Blake. You must be Rick, right?"

He moved forward in greeting, leaving the halo of light behind him. A flesh and blood man now, no longer some angel that just happened to land in her doorway. His forearms, where they emerged from the soft dove grey T-shirt material, were tanned brown. Dark blue jeans clung to his powerful thighs. He moved silently in his running-shoe clad feet. Cripes, he didn't walk, so much as prowl. This guy was one hot, intimidating specimen.

His hand enveloped her smaller one in a firm shake. No one could ever accuse Becky of a weak handshake. It was one of the chief ways she judged a person and, judging from his, he was used to being in control. She gave as good as she got, looking him square in the eye. A strong jaw highlighted a mouth that would make most women wobbly in the knees. His lips were well formed and generous, but there was nothing weak about them. There was nothing weak about *him* in general, she amended. His gaze pierced hers. His eyes drew her in, so dark brown they were almost black in hue.

The feel of his hand, still holding hers, sent icy shivers up and down her arms. Suddenly she felt open and vulnerable, too small next to him. She was used to being the shortest woman in the room, but he made her feel tiny.

He looked down at her with what could only be described as an amused grin. She shifted uncomfortably, pulled her hand from his and motioned to a nearby booth.

Time to stop acting like a dork, Beckers, and interview the stud muffin!

"Have a seat, Rick. Can I offer you something to drink from the bar?" She held her breath. Becky adopted this little test at her grandmother's suggestion. If the prospective employee asked for an alcoholic beverage, she got them out of there fast. Working in a bar was tempting. She had no problem serving her boys on-the-house drinks, but not during working hours and not during an interview. One of the most important parts of the process was weeding out potential problems from the get go.

He appeared to size her up. "No, I'm not thirsty, but thanks anyway." He made himself comfortable in the seat, settled back and waited quietly for her to speak.

Now that he was sitting down she could catch her breath and get a better handle on her wildly spinning emotions. She was surprised by her visceral reaction to this man. She worked with some of the hottest guys in Las Vegas, but none of them had so much as made her look twice. Not even when they stripped to a G-string while they danced on the bar in front of her night after night. This guy, though... He packed a wallop.

His hair, pulled back in a low ponytail, reached just below his shoulder-blades. Loose it would flow over his back in a blue-black cloud. His long fingers were laced together in front of him, and his face seemed relaxed, but a slight wariness in his eyes belied his seeming ease. There was something familiar about the way he moved. The body beneath his clothes reminded her of someone, but she couldn't quite place it. She looked at his face. No, it was a stranger's eyes that assessed her, but still... There, in the movement of his head, the way he cocked it, she was sure she'd seen that before, knew him somehow. Mentally she shook herself, it was time to conduct the interview. Hopefully this guy would work out, even though he was staring at her with an uncomfortable intimacy.

Swallowing hard she looked down at the table to avoid his penetrating gaze. *Get a grip on yourself, Beckers.* She needed something to do with herself or she was never going to get to the interview. Picking up the already familiar application she looked it over once more. Good, now she had a place to start.

51

"So, Rick Frazier, why do you want to be a bartender in a strip club?"

Chapter Six

She didn't wait to get to the heart of the matter, did she? Trying to form a coherent answer to the pointed question, Rick sat back in the comfortable booth and attempted to appear thoughtful.

Mentally he gathered himself. He thought about giving her a glib smart-ass answer, yet the sincerity in her smiling brown eyes stopped him. "Truthfully, I need the money and I have experience as a bartender."

She was tiny, probably no more than five foot two and a hundred and twenty-five pounds dripping wet. A black T-shirt clung to her ample breasts. Her body was generously curvy, but at the same time still taut beneath the casual outfit she wore. Still, it wasn't her lush body that threatened to harden his dick and tent the front of his jeans, it was her heart-stopping face. A perfect oval with huge brown eyes that spoke out eloquently from beneath high arched brows. Her long chestnut brown hair was pulled back with clips, the rest fell down her back in rippling waves. She was a looker all right.

Uh, oh. Danger, Rick Frazier, danger.

Shit, this was a bad time for his mind to wander to sex. This was a job interview, not a date. He'd learned the hard way that attractive women were dangerous. Sure they looked great, too bad they'd put you a on a pedestal and try to turn you into

Prince Charming when you weren't looking. The problem here was, she sure didn't appear one bit helpless like his ex was. Nothing about Becky Blake screamed, "rescue me, big boy". He had little experience with strong women, apart from his mother.

His gaze settled on her lips. What would it be like to have that full, pouting perfection wrapped around his cock, he wondered? He could almost hear the little moans escaping her throat as she sucked him deeper. Feel his hands wrapping themselves in tight fists in her hair, silently urging her to bring him to a mind shattering orgasm.

Mentally he pulled himself back. If she knew what he was thinking he'd be out of here fast. Silently informing his cock to calm the heck down, he concentrated on the color of the booth, then the texture of the table. Anything to control his rabid, drooling libido.

She consulted the application in front of her. Rick clamped down hard on the urge to squirm in his seat like a naughty six-year-old. She was putting him on edge and that was not something he was used to. Normally he was the one with the resume in front of him. He did the grilling. *Ha! Not anymore.* Thanks to Tara, this was his brand new paradigm, like it or not.

"I see your experience ends five years ago. May I ask what you've been doing since then?"

Oh boy. How was he going to answer this one? He didn't want to come off as a know-it-all, kiss-ass, big business schmuck. Honesty was probably the best policy, he reasoned. "For the last five years I owned my own software company. I wrote database programs to track documents for large corporations. I went through a nasty divorce and the company was forced to fold. The truth is, I just need a job 'til I get my new business started. I don't want to waste your time here, Ms.

Blake. This isn't going to be a lifelong career move. I just need the money."

She appeared to think for a moment. "Well, I am looking for someone long term. Look, Rick, I'm sort of in a lurch here. I'm willing to entertain the idea of short-term employment. I guess it all depends how you do on the quiz." Her mouth smiled, but her eyes held a wicked glint.

She slid a paper and pen across the table to him. Reaching out, his fingers brushed hers as he moved to take the printed sheet. Unexpected electric heat arched between them in palpable waves. The gaze that shot to his registered confusion. She pulled back her hand as if burned. Her response did not surprise him. It had taken all his self control not to react the same way to the intense connection at their flesh meeting.

"Um, just let me know when you're ready." Her voice sounded hesitant and soft in his ears.

"Oh, and, Rick?"

He looked up. "Yes?"

"You can call me Becky."

The sultry voice mixed with her peppery smile captivated him. Unable to turn away first, he watched as she stood and returned behind the bar, presumably to finish whatever she'd been doing when he'd walked in.

Fighting to dismiss the warm scent of sandalwood from his mind, her scent, he glanced down at the paper in front of him. It looked like a fifteen question test on how to mix drinks. The majority of them were fruit based. Some were old standbys like Martinis and Cosmos. There was also an essay question about how he would handle a difficult situation. The test seemed to be thorough without being too labor intensive. He had to hand it to her, this was a good way to weed out the riff-raff.

With a soft grunt he began to write, grateful he'd taken some time between code corrections to brush up on his bartender's bible the night before. Some of the questions turned out to be pretty complicated. This job would be nowhere near as easy as slinging beers in the college joint had been. Still, he'd enjoyed his work there. The people he met, the laughter, it had made an otherwise stressful time in his life pleasurable. Maybe bartending would be his lucky penny one more time, helping him survive mentally as well as financially. His gaze locked on the next question. Brows furrowed in concentration as he began to write out the recipe for a Dirty Martini.

With a satisfied smile, he dotted the last period and put down his pencil. "Done."

"Already?" He watched her wipe her small hands, this time on a towel rather than her pants. Too bad, he was having a hard time getting that little gesture out of his mind. Her movements looked like walking sex. Her curvy body flowed along the floor, almost at a glide. He'd think it was practiced, if she didn't seem to do it without any thought. Damn, her gait got under his skin.

He wasn't ready for a repeat performance of that mind-searing touch, so he shoved the paper across the table before she even arrived. She picked it up and began to read over his answers as she sank into the leather booth. He was fairly confident humping her leg like a desperate dog was not going to get him hired. Once more he made a mental note to pick up some lube before he headed home. It looked like the petite brunette would star in his steamy sexual fantasies before morning.

She studied the paper, her smooth brow wrinkled in quiet thought. Every now and then she nodded, then made a notation in red pen. She looked up, smiling. "This is quite good. You forgot the coconut rum in the Bahama Mama, but even I have to look at the recipes every now and then. I like your garnish ideas." Looking at him assessingly, she folded her arms across her chest. "Would you stand up please?"

Shrugging, he scooted out of the booth watching her closely. She was up to something. The telltale blush started slowly at the top of her pretty head and crept down to her pointed little chin.

Her eyes slipped away from his. "I hate to ask this of you... We have a uniform here. Would you mind taking off your shirt?" Her head dipped as she studied the table.

He should have seen this one coming. When he'd entered the place he couldn't miss the wall of muscle-bound men in stark black and white photos. He'd presumed they were the dancers, but whatever flight of the imagination made him think the bartenders would be immune from the same treatment was obviously misguided.

Without a word he drew his shirt from the waistband of his jeans and pulled it over his head in one smooth motion.

He heard her catch of indrawn breath, and even though he should be ashamed of himself for disquieting her, he got a secret thrill out of it. Muscle-wise, he knew he couldn't compete with the wall of hunks out front, still, hours in the apartment building's gym had given him some definition. He didn't want to analyze why he cared so much what this one small woman thought, but it mattered. In some small way her opinion was already important to him.

He gave her what he hoped was a wry smile. "Does this work for you?"

Her mouth, which had been hanging open, clamped shut into a prim little line. Her eyes darted around the room, presumably to look anywhere but at him. "You can get dressed now." Her voice, squeaky and small, made him chuckle inside. It was comforting to know he got to her like she got to him.

Leveling a slow smile in her direction, he complied with her order at a snails pace. There was no need to hurry this reverse striptease along. He had her flustered and, to be honest, it was kind of fun. He had the definite feeling that flustered was not something Becky Blake got very often. She seemed too businesslike and controlled for that.

She looked away, blushing, and bent her head to stare at her nails. He fought not to laugh out loud. What was going to happen if he got the job and worked with her every night, his bare chest exposed? What if the uniform was something even more exotic? Maybe he should clear that up before he took the position, provided it was offered.

I have a few positions I want to get her into.

Damn there was his libido talking again. Which was damn interesting because he hadn't had sexual thoughts about a flesh and blood woman for months. A fantasy built in his mind, sure, but not a real live girl. Imaginary women didn't sleep around behind your back and break your heart.

"Okay, um thank you. Have a seat."

He finished yanking the cotton over his head and sat down to wait while she made more notes on his application.

She looked up with a smile. "Rick, I'd like to offer you the job. Will you join us as our new, temporary, head bartender?"

"May I ask what the job pays first?"

He heard the whispered, "damn" under her breath and smiled sweetly at her. He didn't want to make her miserable and flustered, it just seemed to be happening on its own.

Yeah, but you don't have to enjoy it quite so much.

She put a business face on and straightened her back. "Ten dollars an hour plus gratuities. Most of the guys make a couple hundred a night in tips. You'll be working from six 'til an hour after close, which is two most nights. You get vacation and sick time as well as benefits after the first ninety days. I would like you to work four days a week. Friday and Saturday plus any other two days except Monday, we're closed then." She'd ticked each point off almost mechanically. "Do you have any questions?"

"A couple," he admitted. "I thought most strip clubs in Las Vegas were open till the wee hours?"

She laughed and her eyes lit her face. She became completely relaxed and animated for the first time since he'd met her. "That's the wonderful thing about this place. Our clientele consists mostly of local housewives and out-of-towners having bachelorette parties. A lot of the local ladies have curfews, set by their worried husbands and boyfriends. Most of the other visitors are convention goers with morning meetings or vacationers here to gamble. Even the bridal groups head home around two or so, usually because the bride is three sheets to the wind. You can hear the cell phones start to ring all over the bar about closing time."

He laughed, too. "Get 'em home before they do any real damage, right?"

She nodded.

"Okay, Becky Blake, you have yourself a bartender. When do I start?"

Biting her lip adorably, she stood. "How's tonight working for you?"

"Fine by me. Oh, I almost forgot. What's this uniform you spoke about?"

She grinned evilly at him. "Tight jeans, the tighter the better, the other bartenders will help you zip into them. Cowboys boots, cowboy hat and a leather vest. No shirt. I'll send one of the guys to a western shop with you before we open. It's five now. You might as well stay if you can. I'll have one of the boys show you around. Someone should be here in about ten minutes or so."

A leather vest? She had to be kidding. He gave a shake of his head. My how the corporate had fallen. No wonder she'd needed to leer at his chest. Well no one could say turnabout wasn't fair play, men had ogled women for centuries. He was an official hunk of meat. His mother would have been so proud!

Chapter Seven

"So that's him? Dang, Becky, he's a stud."

Becky took another appreciative sip of the warm herb tea. Five o'clock usually found her sitting in the "The Moon's Daughter" chatting with Vivian. Becky tried to get to the bar around three each day to do her book-work, knocking off for a break with Viv before the staff started trickling in around six. It made for a long day, but running the place was worth it, though.

They were both watching the club's new bartender make his way across the strip-mall parking lot to a small sleek car, Tad in tow. Before heading over to the occult shop, Becky had asked her head bartender to take Rick to a local western wear shop to get the required uniform. He was moving away from them now. His damn amazing ass would look great in the dark denim.

Becky chuckled. "The poor guy has no idea how tight those jeans are that Tad's gonna zip him into tonight."

"You should be ashamed of yourself, you know. You're lucky one of those guys hasn't sued you for cutting off the circulation to his balls and making him sterile," Vivian said with a naughty smile.

Becky gasped. "Damn, Vivian, I can't believe you actually said that." What popped out of the older woman's mouth never ceased to amaze her. "Wait a minute." She pointed an accusing finger. "I seem to remember grandma telling me you two came up with that uniform together and that the tight pants were your special contribution."

Vivian's innocent look did not hide the gleam in her eye. "Who me? I can't seem to remember that, must be getting Alzheimer's."

"Yeah right," Becky snorted out. "Your mind is sharper than mine. What are you now? Fifty?" One foot slipped behind the other as she sent each of her shoes to the floor with a thunk. She hitched her bottom up, drew her feet beneath her and gave the seer a smart assed grin.

"Don't try cute with me, missy. I've been cute for more lives than you can count.

Leaning back into the comfortable chair, Becky smiled and took another sip of tea. She had never ceased to be pleasantly surprised by Vivian's shop. The space was light and airy, with big windows that allowed the warm sunshine to pour into the room. Charming. There were plenty of comfortable nooks for people to curl up in while they perused one of the many books or sipped free samples of Vivian's herbal brews. It sure wasn't what Becky thought of as a typical occult shop. Then again, there was nothing typical about her friend.

A many-times-published author on all matters of modern-day Witchcraft, Vivian was famous in certain circles. She often took off on long weekend getaways to speak at various gatherings around the country, her husband George at her side.

Vivian's sharp gaze leveled on Becky. "So what's eating you? You feel confused to me."

It was amazing the way this woman read her. Becky couldn't figure out how Vivian seemed to get it right every single time. "I don't know, Vivian. There's something about him. I just can't put my finger on it. It's weird, almost as if I know him."

Vivian looked serious. "We all know people from our past lives, Beckers. Surely you've felt these kinds of feelings with people before, haven't you?"

"Well sure, there's you. I felt an immediate connection to you, but other people? No, I can't say it's ever happened before. You know I don't believe in all that past life stuff."

Vivian smiled indulgently at her. "No one's perfect, honey. All I'm saying is this...don't dismiss this feeling. Mr. Hot and Hunky might be here to teach or tell you something." Vivian looked up as the bells on the door jingled. "There's my six o'clock reading, Beckers. You come talk to me tomorrow and let me know how Hot and Hunky did."

Becky chugged the rest of her tea and hunted the floor with her toes, searching for her shoes. "You bet, Viv. Have a good night and say 'hi' to George for me. Don't have too much fun"

Vivian smiled. "George and I always have too much fun. His performance in the sack's the reason we're still married after forty years."

Laughing, Becky stuffed her fingers in her ears as she headed to the exit. "La, la, la, I can't hear you."

ಉ ಲ

"Well?" How am I doin'?"

"Hmmm?" Becky replied distractedly. She'd not been paying one bit of attention to what had come out of Rick's mouth. His biceps, as they strained to lift a plastic case of longnecks, were eye poppingly gorgeous. All her concentration had been focused on those hard sexy muscles. His body proved too much of a diversion for her willpower. She normally helped behind the bar, doing actual work, not staring like a calf-eyed teen at the latest hottie of the month. Her guys counted on her help and she'd never let them down, 'til now. Tonight visual feasting on her new bartender's body in his barely there uniform had been too much of a disruption.

"How-am-I-doing-tonight?" He slowly enunciated every word, presumably because she was acting like a half-wit.

She could feel herself color again. This man sure had a way of making her blush. It sucked. "Great, you're doing great. I can't believe you're staying on top of the orders so well. Keep it up and Tad will be able to leave with a clear conscience."

Turning, she busied herself cutting garnishes, there was always a need to replace the ever dwindling supply. Girlie drinks all seemed to require an amazing array of cut up fruit stuck on top of them.

The tight space behind the bar made for some heart-stoppingly close contact with this gorgeous man. She smiled as she watched him out of the corner of her eye. He leaned forward to take an order from a shockingly clad bottle-blonde wearing a veil on her head. The brides-to-be could be pretty tough on her guys, almost always drunk off their asses and grabby. Each one, it seemed, had an agenda to make the guys want them before they walked down the aisle. More often than not, the poor bartenders got the brunt of it. The strippers could be intimidating to the ladies who frequented the club. The bartenders were somehow more approachable.

One muscular, tanned arm snaked into the ice storage bin next to Becky. He then filled a blender, presumably with the order for the blonde. Looking a little uncomfortable he leaned in. "I seem to be getting a lot of phone numbers tonight. Is that normal?"

She laughed. "Yep, perfectly. What are you doing with them?"

He nodded behind him and to the right.

Glancing back she saw an impressive stack of bar napkins, sticky notes and business cards. She whistled. "Not bad for your first night here, cowboy. Looks like you have your pick of fillies to ride the range with." She should probably try to hide her humor. She glanced at him again. Nope, she couldn't play it straight. Not a chance . The look on his face was damn funny.

Raising an eyebrow he looked down at her meaningfully. "You know that's sexist, right?"

"Yep, it sure is. And your problem with that would be...?"

He burst out laughing. Feminine heads swiveled, the masculine sound catching the attention of most of the ladies at the bar. Well, she amended, he already had their attention, but now they were more blatant about it.

He nodded to indicate the stage. "I've been watching the show all night. I have to say it's been real educational. I never in my life thought I'd see so many out of control women together in one place."

She looked up. Every table and booth was filled with a cross section of the ladies of Las Vegas. Some visitors, some locals. The mix included business suits, polyester pants outfits straight off Carol Brady's back, low cut numbers that left little to the imagination and blue jean types. Ages ran the gamut as well. Her club thrived on diversity.

"This?" She frowned, her arm sweeping over the bar complete with bobbing celery stalk in hand. "This is a pretty quiet night. We haven't had to call the bouncer into anything yet. Sometimes these ladies get really wild."

He looked at her in what could only be described as disbelief. "You're kidding right? Bouncers for this crowd?" His eyes appeared to zero in on a table of screaming women in "mom jeans".

She nodded to one of the back corners. "See the guy in the Stetson over there?"

Rick followed her gaze.

"Name's 'Muscles'. He does our bouncing."

"Him? He's huge. He doesn't hurt the ladies when he boots them, does he?" Concern edged his voice.

"Nope, Muscles wouldn't hurt a fly. He usually sweet talks them right out the door. He even has his own fan website of loyal followers."

The lights dimmed, then flashed brighter before dimming once again.

"Uh oh, gotta go do my thing. Hold down the fort." She tossed a towel at Rick and headed for the stage.

This part of the job had been the hardest for Becky to learn, speaking to the crowd of ladies, working them up to a loosely controlled frenzy when she introduced special acts. As she reached the stage, her hand connected with the mike offered by the D-jay. Flipping it on, she stepped into the hot blazing lights.

"Hey Lad-ies, How're you all doin' tonight? Are you ready to show some real appreciation for our incredibly sexy men?" The crowd of women roared. "Let's show our hardworking drink servers and bartenders some love ladies. Can I hear it for the boys? Boys wave to the lovely ladies." Arms went up all through the place as the cowboy look-a-likes waved to the screaming throng.

Becky smiled big. She probably should have warned Rick. He seemed like a nice guy, too bad for him that this hazing was something all the new guys went through when they joined the team. It was damn mean, entertaining and funny as hell. Every one of the employees kept the initiation a secret. She considered it to be a bonding experience.

"We have a *very* special treat for you tonight, ladies, a brand new bartender, Rrriiiiccckkk! Come on up here, Rick, and show these ladies what you've got."

She waited. She knew he'd be there. On his own or carried by six burly strippers. No one got out of this abuse.

"I don't think he feels the love, ladies. Let's hear it for him. Come on, let's see if we can't make him a little less shy. We don't want a bashful bartender, now do we?" The crowd went wild.

Out of the corner of her eye she saw movement beyond the first row. The lights made it almost impossible to see more than a few feet into the audience, which helped the guys perform unselfconsciously. The commotion grew closer. Sure enough, there was her new bartender being carried onto the stage, hefted by four muscle bound Adonis look-a-likes. She was relieved to see he was smiling. Some guys didn't go along with this, but if they wanted to make the good tips they had to make the crowd believe that they were available and eager for the attention they received. The burly strippers dumped Rick's unresisting body on the stage. Standing, he smiled and gave an embarrassed wave to the audience.

"Okay, ladies, here he is. Let's welcome him aboard, and, Rick baby? You can leave your hat on."

The song of the same name, timed to coincide with her words, filled the space with an inviting beat. Beneath her booted feet the floor vibrated to the deep base.

Becky tried not to laugh as Rick stood there for a few moments blinking under the heat of the lights, the crowd of frenzied women going bonkers at his feet. She held her breath, waiting to see what his reaction would be. He looked back at Becky with a withering glance, shrugged, then spun a tight turn. Frenzied encouragement from the crowd seemed to make him lose all inhibitions. Soon he was all smiles as he danced.

From her vantage point next to the D-jay booth, Becky had a terrific view of the hot bartender's moves. He writhed sinuously for the screaming women. One his powerful hands reached to his hair, pulling the mass free of the ponytail he'd worn all night, his movement's hypnotic as he stripped his vest from his body in one savage movement. His hips slipped like he'd stripped his entire life. The room seemed to shrink to just the two of them. Her breasts swelled, almost to the point of aching, the muscles at the apex of her thighs tightening in response to his every move.

She smiled out at the audience. It was important that she maintained an air of interest without any actual drool landing on the floor in front of her. Peeking at his body out of the corner of her eye, she fought her desire to just blatantly stare and damn the consequences.

Tipping his hat forward, Rick turned from the audience, giving them a sexy view of his muscular ass while the full heat of his gaze landed on Becky. She'd never felt weak in the knees before. Not in her life. This man, she fanned herself, he was heat personified.

The music ended, the torture cut mercifully short by her D-jay. Removing his hat, Rick turned to face the audience, bowing low to thunderous applause as his hair covered his face. Dollar bills rained onto the stage. Becky looked on, trying to squash her libido. Her heart beating lightening fast, her mouth without moisture. There was no way in hell she could put together a sensible patter.

Preparing to speak once more, she looked up as Rick turned to give the crowd another look at his backside. Becky's world reduced to a black tunnel, devoid of sound save for the memory of the coyote's howl. Breath exited her lungs in a *woofff* as shocked recognition flooded over her in a dizzy wash. Without the hat, his long black hair haloing the hawk-like features of his face tripped her memory. Like a camera set to auto-focus, muted impressionist features sharpened into startling detail. Rick Frazier was the coyote man from her dream.

Chapter Eight

Shit. No wonder he'd looked so familiar to her. After Rick finished his dance, Becky made a beeline for her office. A phone call to Viv was her first priority. She needed her friend now. Her hands trembled as she punched the buttons and drew the phone to her ear. One ring, then two. The same sound repeated over and over again as frustration forced her feet to pace back and forth in the small space. The woman probably *was* psychic, Becky conceded, but that didn't replace an answering machine.

How the hell could she have had a sexual dream about a man she'd never seen before and have the man end up in her bar the very next night? Yes, she'd cast the spell, but in her heart did she think it would work? Did she believe? She squeezed her eyes tight with the fingers of her free hand. Confusion clouded her brain, she couldn't think straight.

"Come on, Viv, pick up. Please pick up. I really need to talk to you now. Stop playing nookie-muffins and answer the damn phone." Pleading did not seem to help. The persistent ring continued to jangle in her ear. *Fine.* She slammed the useless excuse for a cordless wonder down hard. A lock of hair tickled her nose and she twisted the strand into her mouth, sucking the ends. Bleh. Disgusted, she pulled the hair out with a frown. She hadn't bothered with that nasty habit since the fourth grade. Her nerves must be fried, completely shot.

Sweet mother of holy crap. How the hell could she have dreamed about someone whom she'd never so much as seen before? How the heck was that possible?

She stopped her pacing in an effort to focus on her options. A quick glance out the two-way mirror gave her a good idea of what was going on at the bar. He was out there, joking around with the women, bartending his hot, Coyote Man, ass off. What looked to be fifty ladies had all flocked to the oak bar to get a personal pour from the fresh meat. The tip jar was full to almost overflowing.

Well good for him. Those boys deserved good money.

He was so adorably spicy.

What if sex with him was as good as the dream?

No, she was not going to go there. Not at all. Screwing her employees was strictly off limits.

Your grandmother did it. She's in Italy right now getting her seventy-three-year-old brains fucked out by a man less than half her age.

The red devil on her shoulder was having some fun now. She'd smack it if she thought for one moment it was real, not that it would do any good at all. She had a definite feeling that the teeny bugger would enjoy being smacked around a little too much.

Don't look now, Beckers, that sexy beast is headed this way.

Yep, Coyote Man was headed right for her door. The knock sounded loud in the small room as it reverberated off the flocked walls.

"Come in." She had to get it together here. She was acting like a moron.

"Becky? Tad said to tell you that he didn't know which hole you disappeared into, but it's almost time for last call."

She took a deep breath, letting it out a bit at a time. Plastering on a big fake smile, she turned to answer him. "Okay, Rick. Tell Tad I'll be right there."

"Sure thing, boss."

The door closed behind him. She'd better find a way to get her equilibrium back, fast. She considered her options. She could fire him. That might work. What would she say? *"Gee you look just like a guy who brought me to orgasm in a dream and I'm deathly afraid of screwing the people I work with. Since I might jump your hump at any moment, I'm letting you go for your own good."* Yeah that would go over real nice. Drat that Vivian anyway. Becky was in over her head and needed help here. You'd think a psychic would know when to answer the damn phone.

You know, you could just go out there, act normally and see what happens. Maybe he really is the man you conjured, ever think of that, missy?

Great, the teensy red moron had elected to be logical. She could never resist logic. *Why not?* Why not just go out there and act like she hadn't imagined Rick Frazier rubbing his cock over her thigh in her dreams and see what happened? So she was attracted to him? So what? She bet lots of women were. She peered out the two-way again, her eyes searching for his face. He was surrounded. The ladies practically clawed their way over one another to get near him. Only Tom, the ten inch wonder sitting in the photographer's chair in a miniscule G-string with women draped all over his lap, was receiving more attention. Still, when she really compared them, Tom's queue of hungry fans and the long line of women trying to get one more drink from the sexy bartender were about even. Yep, he was getting plenty of attention alright.

She couldn't hide in her office forever, even if she wanted to. For one thing she had to use the lady's room. The other was the office bore a frightening resemblance to a bad interior decorator's idea of a nineteen-seventies bordello. Her grandmother had odd taste in décor, and the room gave Becky a headache. Better to go out there and deal with the man like an adult woman.

Yeah, that's right. Jump him like the sex God he is.

Damn, that voice had better shut up quick. This was not the time for sarcastic crap. Maybe she *was* going crazy. That'd be great. She could go for a nice rest in a mental hospital and forget all about the Hunk-O-Rama and his dramatic transformation in the desert.

ഇ രു

Leaning over the bar to take what had to be the millionth phone number of the evening, Rick smiled politely as the well-dressed woman mouthed, "call me", her pinky and thumb stretched to her ear to mimic a phone. This was exactly like being the star of a bad seventies sexploitation pic, he marveled. The whole bizarre experience could be titled, "Night of the Hungry Women". No, that wasn't quite right, maybe, "Night of the Sex Starved She-Beasts". Now *there* was a marquee. Much better. That one definitely had the right tone.

Glancing back at the mirror that covered one wall of Becky's office, his eyes were drawn to the door as an elfin face popped out and looked suspiciously around. She'd been acting oddly since his strip tease, but she was still adorable. He tried to hide an enthusiastic smile as she came towards the bar.

Becky Blake sure was easy on his eyes, even though she looked tired now, her eyelids drooping. He wondered if she always worked such long hours. Judging from the stack of applications in the "no" pile he'd seen today, she must have come in at the butt crack of dawn.

There was something about her that made him instantly comfortable in her presence. Like he'd known her forever. If anyone could break his self imposed celibacy, it would be Becky Blake. He grinned, maybe it was time to think about retiring Rosy and explore this new prospect. Still, it sure didn't feel like they'd met only a few hours before. More like he'd known her for years. Great, now he was thinking like one of those desperate folks he'd seen heading into the Occult shop next door. Not exactly his style.

"Hey guys, you 'bout ready to call it a night?"

Her voice all honey and cream as she stood next to him, she held one slender hand poised over the light switch. The murmured affirmatives all around had her moving her hand upwards, bringing the lights above the bar to an almost daylight level. Then she dimmed them once again. This was a last reminder to the ladies that their night of fun was about to come to an end.

On cue the D-jay picked up the microphone. "Well that's it ladies. Thank you for joining all our hot, hot men at the Buckin' Bronco tonight. From all of our fifty wonderful dancers, our amazing bartenders, and the rest of the staff, we'd like to thank you most kindly for giving us a visit. Get on home safe and sound and be sure and come back real soon, ya'll hear?"

A sad "aww" rose from the floor as the remaining clientele prepared to call it a night or move on to other venues. Muscles appeared to be talking to some of the more inebriated of the bunch.

"They'll get home okay?" Rick asked.

"Them? Oh sure. Muscles will call them cabs on us if they can't get home another way. Their cars are fine, the parking lot's patrolled all night by our security. They'll be all right."

He watched her say goodnight to some of the patrons, calling many by name, hugging a few more. She seemed comfortable talking to them, almost like she knew them well. She must have read his mind because she smiled one of those heart-stoppers he'd seen her give all night.

"I love this place. You'll get to know the regulars pretty quickly. Most of them are nice women who are just lonely or have husbands that aren't around for one reason or another. I don't judge them, just make sure they have a damn good time."

"You really seem to care about them." He watched the emotions play across her face. Kindness, caring and love reflected in her eyes.

She considered his words with a tilt of her head. "Yeah, I do. They're all wonderful. They accepted my takeover without question. Their loyalty pushes me to make their experience here memorable."

"Takeover?" He'd been curious how a sweet woman with a flat Midwestern accent ended up in Vegas owning a strip club.

She looked up into his eyes and he felt his toes go numb. "It used to my grandmother's. She fell in love with one of the strippers, a thirty-eight-year-old. They're in Italy right now, but next month they go on an around the world cruise."

Snapping his jaw shut with a little click, he looked at her in disbelief. "I don't mean to insult you, but you're not nineteen, how old is your grandmother?"

She laughed. "Old enough. She started young, then my parents started young. I'm considered an old maid in my family." She arched a wry brow. "I'm thirty one."

He whistled. "Dang. That's some dame."

Her face lit with joy. "Yep, she sure is. There's a book to be written there, I think."

She turned as the first of the strippers walked past. "Night, Tom. Hug Grace and the boys for me will you?"

He watched the tall man turn, his grin genuine. "You betcha, Beckers. Tell granny I said, 'hi' the next time you talk to her."

"Will do."

She turned back to Rick. "Did you get a chance to meet Tom tonight?"

Rick shook his head. "I was too busy. I do remember you introducing him by another name though."

"Yep." She smirked. "'Ten Inch Tom'. You'd never guess from watching him work that he's a grad student with three boys all under four, would you?"

"Wow, amazing." He blew out an incredulous breath.

"Some of the guys are family men, most are students just trying to pay their own way. Now, why don't I show you how to clean this place up?"

They worked for another hour to get the bar set up and ready for an always rowdy Saturday night. Rick's body felt almost in pain. Every time the woman accidentally brushed against him, or stood on tiptoes to re-rack the glasses, showing her ass to advantage, was nothing less than torture. His cock strained in the too-tight jeans. All he could wrap his brain around was the sexy thought of stripping off her clothes, laying her across the bar and fucking her senseless.

The sweet smiles she gave to every one of the guys weren't helping any. He imagined her smiling for him alone, those gorgeous legs wrapped around his waist. She was fire and he wanted to burn up in her embrace. For some reason he kept fantasizing about her body surrounded by candle flame, naked and wanting, stretched out before him. This was agony. As surreptitiously as he could, he shifted his cock, trying to make it more comfortable in the denim prison.

It was just about three a.m. now and he was beat. His eyes were scratchy and raw, his muscles drained of energy. They'd sent Tad home half an hour ago, but Rick still had the stocking to do. At this moment his new boss was stretched out over the bar, her enticing ass in the air as she wiped the sleek oak surface down with a bleach rag. The picture she presented was enough to make a grown man cry.

She wiggled her hips in a fascinating display as she scooted back. He watched her stretch her feet towards the ground, toes searching uselessly three inches short of the rubber coated floor. He told himself he was just lending the new boss a hand as he reached his arms to her. Just being a stand up guy. The truth was he couldn't have stopped himself if he'd tried. Grasping her curvy hips between his hands he drew her back, by tender inches, against him. Her ass crushed seductively to his stomach, then slid down over his cock, leaving it hard and aching in the wake of her softness.

He felt her body still, heard the hiss of a sharply indrawn breath. The seductive slide complete, she stood on the floor, back pressed to him, constrained against the length of his unyielding body. His chin rested on the top of her head, brushed against her soft hair. Her scent surrounded him, filling his brain with sandalwood and warm woman. He wrapped one arm possessively around her waist and bent his head to press his lips to her neck. For a fraction of a second he hesitated, wondering how she would react. Would she allow this moment? His breath reverberated against the closeness of her skin, heating his face, and the soft warmth of her flesh filled his nostrils with her scent. Just one taste of this woman. Just a soft sweet kiss on her neck and he could control the restless, urgent need to take her that writhed within him.

He pressed his lips against her and the tip of his tongue darted out to taste her silken skin. She moaned, pushing the soft curves of her body against him, womanly and sweet. His hand dipped lower, down over her slightly curved tummy to the soft place between her jean-clad thighs. Rough texture and damp fabric met his questing fingers. She was wet for him, wanted him. He felt a primal urge to yell in triumph, rip the clothing from her, bend her over the bar and fill her body with his.

"Becky?" The whispered word sounded harsh and intrusive in the moment, but he didn't want to fill her with regret later. He needed her permission to continue this sweet assault.

"Yes."

She writhed in his arms, pressed her hot wet crotch against his hand. His other arm still imprisoned her around the waist, holding her as still as possible. Throwing her head back into his chest she rubbed her ass against his hard cock. Sexy moans slipped from her, driving his need to a frenzy of passion.

"Becky, are you all right?" a male voice called to her from across the room.

"Shit." She whimpered and pulled away from him, ripping herself from his arms. It left them feeling cold and empty.

"Yes, I'm fine Muscles. Just finishing up here." She sounded stressed and unnerved, as he would have sounded if he could speak.

"Okay, Becky. I'll just head out then."

Her face red, she hung her head, not looking at the bouncer. "Sounds good to me. See you tomorrow night." The words rang with false cheer.

"Um, Rick, you can go home now. Thanks for the good work tonight."

Dismissed, pushed away. It was obvious he was no longer welcome to touch her. The tone of her voice made her intent clear. His hard throbbing cock begged him to argue, begged him to seduce this woman. He felt like it would explode from the attention it had received from the softest part of her. Too bad he couldn't begin to think about forming words into sentences. Discussion on this matter would not be possible. How did she manage to sound so business-like? Hurt, hauntingly familiar and unwelcome, clogged his throat.

Did she do this with all the new employees?

"See you tomorrow?" A smile hovered at the corners of her mouth, tremulous and apologetic.

Watching her closely, he saw her gaze meet his, then she visibly winced. The pain he suffered had registered with her. Whatever the petite beauty was up to, he felt sure this hadn't been a planned seduction.

Walk away, Frazier. She may want you, but she's not ready. Let her make the next move... or not.

"Six on the dot?" She said it with obvious forced brightness.

Her eyes were still a bit unfocused, giving her a slightly lost appearance. Leaning forward, Rick tilted her mouth to his and planted a quick kiss on her lips. Her eyes became startled and doe-like.

"Six on the dot, Becky."

Whistling the tune he had danced to, he grabbed his hat and boogied out of the bar.

Chapter Nine

Looking up from cleaning the beer taps, Becky watched the silent progress of her smoking new bartender across the club's floor.

Right on time, figures.

Half of her had been hoping he wouldn't show up today so she could fire his tasty ass. No such luck. She was going to have to face the man. She thought about heading to her office to hide, letting the bartenders get ready for the night without her, but that was the coward's way out, and Becky Blake was no coward. Okay, maybe she was a bit of a coward. She'd managed to avoid him for a week, between book work and days off, but it was Friday night. The bar would be too busy for Becky to play childish games.

Once more she smoothed the denim of her way too short skirt. Fussing at her appearance.

Another brilliant idea gone awry, Beckers. You look like a teenage boy's wet dream. Which wouldn't be bad if you were trying to attract a pimply faced youth, but that's just gross.

She couldn't believe she was in the middle of a dumb ass push-pull game. Normally she had no patience for the type of woman who put everything into her looks to attract a man, then cutely pretend he didn't exist in hopes that she'd gain his favor. Now she'd turned into one of those women.

Standing in front of her bedroom mirror for over an hour, she'd tried on every pair of jeans, every top, and every pair of marginally comfortable high heels she owned. A tragically useless attempt to make her ass look smaller and her boobs bigger. All of it to impress the man she was now contemplating running away from like a scared little mouse trying to avoid ingestion by a snake. A damn huge snake she amended, thinking about his cock between her ass cheeks last Friday night.

Her mind had rerun the scene that had played out last weekend. Every time she thought about those strong hands on her body she could feel her pussy swell with need. There was something about this man that just completely got to her, undid her thought processes. She kept catching herself watching him with what she was pretty sure was drool on her lips. At one point, last night, her mouth had actually been hanging open. It wasn't till Muscles walked by and gently lifted her chin back in place that she "got it". In the term of an English Romance Novel she was, "making a cake of herself". A big ole vanilla cake with a ton of Rick Frazier frosting on it and a side of eight-hour sex marathon.

Yum.

That would be fun, hours and hours of incredible sack time with Rick. Cripes, she needed to buy a new vibrator, well that, or get Rick into bed with her. What the hell *were* her plans anyway? She'd never slept with an employee before, never thought about it one time, well maybe once, but the thought had been passing at best. This job made it easy to understand why doctors never got turned on by their patients. After a while, a body really was just a body. Unless it was attached to Rick's brain, yowza. There was truly something special about the man.

Heading right for her he smiled, crinkles forming at the corners of his eyes. He looked truly happy to see her. His long hair, loose for the moment, gleamed around his shoulders. His body in the relaxed fit jeans he wore looked just as hot as it did when he wore the painted on uniform, maybe hotter.

"Hi, Becky. How're you doing tonight?"

Oh, just fine for a woman in heat.

"Great, Rick. Had a good day?" She was a walking ball of entertainment tonight. Talk about your lame-o conversation starters. Nervously she played with the hem of her skirt, trying to pull it lower over her legs.

"Yeah, I got a lot of work done on my program." He leaned close, speaking in a conspiratorial whisper. "You look amazing tonight. Skirts are great on you. They make your legs look gorgeous."

The lascivious gleam in his eye was unmistakable. She was about to turn around and run to her office to hide once again, but that damn devil on her shoulder poked her with that fucking annoying pitchfork.

Sure, you could turn around and run or you could take a chance, doofus. Take the freaking chance. He's obviously attracted to you.

"Um, thanks, I wore it for you." She lowered her chin to stare at the floor.

There it was, hanging out there like a wad of toilet paper stuck to a shoe. It was all up to him now.

His eyes widened as he pulled back, staring intently at her face. "Seriously, you wore that for me? I'm flattered, you look great."

"Really?" She brightened, let go of her hem and stood straight. "I'm glad you like it. You really do?"

"Yes," he said with a laugh. "I love it. I'm grateful you did that for me, Becky. I think you're an astounding woman."

"Hey, Rick, get your butt in here and let's get your uniform on," a disembodied voice yelled from the dressing room.

Damn Tad. He could leave tonight as far as she was concerned.

"Crap, I gotta run, Becky, but do you want to catch some breakfast after closing?"

Was he asking her out? It sure sounded like it. She couldn't remember the last time anyone had done that. She'd been so busy putting out back-off vibes for the last few years she'd rarely been asked out, and never by someone as commanding and sexy as Rick Frazier. She felt like her heart might thump right out the front of her tight black T-shirt. Her fingers drifted back to the hem of her skirt. She was going to wear the material out if she wasn't careful.

"I'd like that, Rick. Thanks." She dropped her gaze from his, turning back to the dirty beer taps with a grin as he sauntered off to the dressing room.

She had a date. She had a date with the guy she'd conjured in the desert.

Yippee!

She was pretty sure she was grinning from ear to ear 'cause her cheeks hurt.

Chapter Ten

Later, Becky felt about as alive as the towels she mopped the bar with and just about as disposable. Grab a cloth, wipe the bar, toss it in the linen pile, grab another one. Yep, that pretty much described her state of mind. It was one of those nights that just wore the life right out of her.

Two bachelorette groups had been in, which was not normally a problem. Her guys knew how to handle the engaged women, making each one feel unique on her special night. The issue arose when the two brides started fighting over "Ten Inch Tom". Each vied for his affections with large bills dangled from perfectly manicured fingertips. Starting as a shouting match, it soon escalated to an all out bridal brawl. Before Becky could get between them, the brides and their parties were going at it on the floor.

Rick and Muscles had taken the brunt of it. In a flash, Rick had been over the top of the bar, separating the two women wearing condom covered veils with his strong arms. Muscles stepped in and talked them both down, in fact he was well on his way to soothing their ruffled feathers with a round of drinks on the house when a maid of honor erupted out of nowhere, scratching and clawing at the opposing bride.

It was a hair pulling, bra strap grabbing, knock down, drag out, two teeth loosened, good ole time. The guys had been quick, but two determined, stressed out brides and their emotionally abused bridal parties had been quicker. In the end the police had been called, statements made and two brides looked like they might be more than late to their own weddings. Where was the Jerry Springer crew when you needed them?

Becky wanted to put her head down on the bar and cry. Grandmother Lucy warned her about nights like this. Thankfully, they were few and far between. Bawling not being an option, she sucked it up as best she could and continued to wait on her other patrons with a smile. The fight seemed to have the effect of dousing cold water on the remaining ladies. At last call, there were few women to gently shoo out the door.

"Penny for your thoughts?" Rick leaned in close as he poured ice into one of the chillers from a big white bucket, the sound of his voice nearly drowned out by the chunking of the frozen cubes. He'd changed into a T-shirt and looser pair of jeans. His ass still filled them out in the most distracting way possible.

"No thoughts really. I'm just wiped out." She yawned, quickly covering her open mouth with her hand.

"You look more beat up than our brides-to-be."

She rolled her shoulders. "That would pretty much explain how I feel right now."

"Do you wanna take a pass on later?"

Later? The date, oh shit, how could she have forgotten her date with Rick? "No, I don't want to do that, but I'm so tired."

He looked at her assessingly. "You know, I think I have an idea. Trust me?"

Cocking an eyebrow, she smiled up at him. "Said the spider to the fly. What do you have in mind?"

He leaned seductively towards her and his hot breath tickled her ear, sending heat all through her body. "That's a secret. Can I run out for a bit?"

Dumbly, she nodded. Chills rolled through her veins leaving raw need behind. The incredible sexiness of this man could definitely be used as a foolproof way to loosen the tongue of an enemy. Ten minutes with Rick and female spies would talk, no doubt about it.

Winking, he headed to the back room, ice bucket swinging in his hand.

With a shake of her head, she turned back to re-stock the clean glasses. This man completely wiped out her inhibitions. When faced with his deep brown eyes and sexy smile, her good intentions melted like ice cream dropped onto a hot sidewalk.

Why is this so damn hard? Just let go and feel, Becky. Isn't this what you dreamed of?

She wanted a relationship, didn't she? Wasn't that why she cast that circle in the desert in the first place? Maybe she was just scared? Well, *there's* a ring of truth in the dark of the night. Duh. Of course she was scared. How many relationships had she been in? Two? That sounded about right, and neither of them had lasted longer than a couple months.

In college she'd been too driven, too focused on her degree, trying for the best grades possible to maintain her scholarship. Ensuring her future success had been her battle cry. The few guys she did date were for a physical release. She'd not felt a real connection with any of them. After college it had been her job. Buying a home with views of the lake had become another priority. Her condo had been nice, but not exactly cuddly on a cold night.

One after another she'd watched her friends don a pure white dress and march down the aisle. She'd told herself that they were leaning on a man, but that had been a copout. Ouch, that revelation hurt. There was truth there, though. A lot of it.

Lost in thought she finished her prep work for the next day on autopilot, barely registering the departure of the guys as they left for the night. Usually she was the last one out. Being alone in the place always made her feel small, but satisfied. Packed with people the club seemed almost cozy, the stage close. By herself, the space felt cavernous. Her gaze traveled from the stage to the tables, moving on to the booths in the back where the guys danced on them tables for the ladies.

All this was hers. Becky smiled. This place was her idea of heaven on earth. Sure, it was noisy, smelled like old beer and baby oiled men, but it she loved it. Every crazy, drunk woman patron, each and every stripper—no matter how ego-maniacal—and each one of the bartenders, gave her a sense of purpose. Then there was Rick, Coyote Man. How did he figure into her private idea of paradise?

A change in air pressure heralded the return of Rick. The aroma proceeding the bags of food he hauled in was beyond enticing. Her stomach rumbled loudly. Pressing two hands over the noisy traitor, she bit her lip in embarrassment. What the heck? She normally never hid her appetite in front of a man. She ate what she ate without picking for the sake of making her date feel like a "real man".

"Here you go, breakfast. Where do you want the food? Your office?"

"Good grief no. I can't eat in there." She shuddered.

He laughed. "I was wondering about that. It doesn't exactly look like the real you."

"How about a booth?" Arm raised, she indicated the coziest of the semi-private booths that perched along the wall near the stage.

"Sounds good to me." He looked back over his shoulder, grinning as he caught her in the act of staring at his ass again. She blushed. "You coming, Becky?"

"Wild horses couldn't keep me away. I'm starved." Race walking was not normally her sport, but the fabulous fragrance was too luscious to resist. Anything that smelled good over stale bar odors had to be delicious. She hurried after him.

She watched him lay out what appeared to be a feast on the smooth table top. His body bent enticingly over the slick surface. The hard muscles, under his tight T-shirt looked almost more delicious than the food.

"I hit the Peppermill. Their stuff's fantastic and the portions are huge. I didn't know what you wanted. I hope semi-Mexican's okay. Do you have plates?"

"What?" Damn, he'd caught her ogling his ass again.

Grinning lecherously at her, he pointed to the food. "Plates, you know, round flat things you put food on, maybe some silverware? That is unless you'd rather eat with your fingers. Which might be more interesting come to think of it."

"Very funny. Yes, I have plates. I was so hungry I spaced it. Hang on a sex, I mean sec."

She felt the heat rise in her body from the toes on up. She'd just bet her face was beet red. Turning, she scurried into the relative safety of her office to blush in private. She grabbed two forks, a couple of plates and a stack of napkins she kept in a drawer. As she passed the bar on the way back, she grabbed two Mexican beers to complete their meal.

"Here ya go. Hope beer's okay." Her voice sounded breathless, on edge. She didn't want to make any more verbal blunders tonight. Rick had a way of making her feel like a giddy teenager in the throes of her first crush.

His eyes twinkled. Great, he thought she was a hoot. Their first date was going to be their last. Not unheard of, but why with this super hot guy? Crud.

"Beer sounds good. Have a seat. What do you want to try first?"

Her eyes traveled over him then moved to the boxes littering the table. The display made her eyes widen. Yum, food first, Rick later. Burritos, nachos, guacamole, salsa and enough chips to feed the entire line up of strippers were all laid out in a tempting array.

"A little of everything please, if that's okay with you?"

He laughed. "You don't need my permission to eat, Becky. That's why I picked it up. It was a hell of a night. Hand me your plate." He plucked the plate from her nerveless fingers with a smile. His capable hands spooned what looked like a mound of food onto her plate, soon filling it to almost overflowing.

Taking the too full plate from him, she placed it in front of her and prepared to dig in, too hungry to care about dignity. With surgical precision she carefully slit the burrito down the middle and laid it wide open. She covered the insides with guacamole and salsa in neat rows, then ran her fork around the inside edges, scooping a bit of all the flavors into one bite. Licking her lips in anticipation, she lifted the colorful mass towards her mouth, only to stop midway as she caught his shocked gaze.

"Umm, is there a problem?"

"No, it's just—well... I've just never seen anyone do that to a burrito before. It's a hell of a way for the poor guy to die."

She laughed. "I've been eating them this way as long as I can remember. My mom did it too. I didn't mean to ick you out."

"No, that's okay. You can eat strangely. I won't tell a soul. I'd hate to be subject to the same treatment. Your secret's safe." He smiled.

She grinned and popped the bite into her mouth, savoring the fresh flavor of avocado and warm cheese. "Mmm, thanks, Rick, this is great. I've ordered in after work before, even gone out with the guys, but I have to admit this is a first. A date in a bar." Smiling around a mouthful of guacamole, she waved her fork, indicating the food. "We'll never be able to do justice to this mountain you brought back."

"Oh yeah? Watch me. I can eat." He wasn't lying either. Already he was reaching for more nachos. "So, tell me about that office of yours. It's not quite...well, you."

Making a face, she looked back at the door of what she thought of as her den of inequity. "It's not, grandma designed it. She's a great old gal, but her taste all runs to early bordello. I've made a lot of changes to the décor since I took over, but not the office. I thought removing the cherubs from the lady's room was a higher priority."

Eyes wide, he appeared awed. "You're kidding right?"

"Nope, I kid you not. Purple wallpaper, gold cherubs and pink sinks. The wallpaper was even flocked. She got her inspiration on a tour of the Liberace Museum she took one day. She was in love with Liberace. You should have heard her the day they announced he died." She shuddered in mock horror.

"She knows he was gay right?"

"Shhh, no she does not and no one has the guts to tell her."

"No offense to your grandma, but that's kind of hard to miss. It's been in all the papers."

"What can I say? She's in deep denial. I love her anyway. Come to think of it, the guy she ran off with looks like a young Liberace."

90

He laughed. "That's priceless. Do you miss her?"

"Nope. I see her about as much as ever. I was living in Chicago before she ran off. We talk on the phone once or twice a week and she's the original e-mail queen."

Cocking an eyebrow, he studied her intently, making her squirm in her seat. "You moved all the way from Chicago to run The Buckin' Bronco? Do you miss your old life?"

Considering, she took a long sip of her beer. *Delicious.* "Surprisingly, no. I don't miss the winter, that's for sure. I haven't been here through a summer yet, so I have no clue what I'm in for. And I have more friends here than I did in the corporate world. I worked all the time, even when I was home. Here, well the hours suck, but I love it even so. Las Vegas is great."

He grinned and his eyes lit up. "I love it here too. You're in for it when summer arrives, otherwise it's still pretty wonderful. The sunsets are stunning."

"So I take it you're not a native either?"

Shaking his head, he reached for the nape of his neck and slid the black elastic from his hair, loosening it. He dropped the band to the table and used the fingers of both hands to shake his hair out. How would it feel to have that thick mass brush her thighs?

Becky swallowed hard, the itch to run her hands through the shiny strands almost stronger than she could stand.

"I'm just a small town boy from southeastern Montana. Went to college in California and settled in San Francisco with my ex. I came out to Las Vegas after the divorce." He didn't look comfortable discussing this. No longer meeting her eyes, he studied his empty plate as if it contained all the secrets of the universe.

She should probably drop it, let the whole thing go and change the subject. Who was she kidding? Since when did she listen to common sense? "Why Vegas?"

He shrugged. "I was angry. I came home early to a bad scene. I just stormed out. I got in my car and drove, headed south along the California coastline till I realized that my life had been all about pleasing my clients to make money to support Tara, that's my ex. I spent my whole life trying to be the perfect corporate do-gooder. I was so busy trying to prove I was as smart as the next guy that I lost myself. I made a left at L.A. and headed east. When the sun came up I was in Las Vegas. It seemed like a good place to stop. I went back to straighten things out, meet my obligations, but this town became my refuge. It felt like a good place to call home. No bad memories, no pain, enough people to get lost in the crowd and get some time to think."

He hesitated for a moment, then continued, "It's the fastest growing city in the US. I figured this would be a good place to start over. I think a lot of people do."

Becky nodded. "I understand. So what about your family? Are they around?"

He winced.

"Is that a touchy subject? I didn't mean to pry."

"Yes, but it's a fair question. Dad was never in the picture. Mom met him in college, got pregnant with me and went home to her parents. They're traditionalists, and having a child with an absent father, one who was not raised in our culture, was a no, no. She was pretty much on her own most of my life. She worked hard to give me more than she'd had. She died from complications of diabetes a couple years ago."

"Oh, Rick, I am so sorry."

He titled his head. "It happens. Instances of adult onset diabetes are pretty high where I'm from."

She wanted to hold him. Make it better. It was obvious he was hurting inside and that this conversation was hard for him. She'd been a bitch to push it.

He took a deep breath. "So, what about you. What's the real history of Becky Blake, Chicago girl turned bar owner?"

Now it was her turn to feel uncomfortable. She clasped her hands under the table. "There's not much to it. My mom died when I was sixteen, hit by a car. Dad sort of fell apart, she'd been his whole world. He committed suicide a year later. Grandma Lucy is the only family I have left, except for Vivian."

"Who's she?"

"The owner of, "The Moon's Daughter" next door."

"You mean the spook spot?" His brow furrowed.

Becky laughed. "I take it you're not a true believer?"

He grinned. "Me? Nope, I'm not discounting it, but it seems some of her clientele are a bit on the fringe. If you know what I mean."

She thought for a moment. "I guess some of her clients are pretty desperate, but there does seem to be something to what she does over there. Viv gives good people hope for a bright tomorrow." She looked down.

"Oops, did I just offend you?"

She brightened. "No, not really, it takes all kinds and I have a hard time with some of Viv's beliefs too. I still adore her though, and she loves me, even though I'm a skeptic. Wow, look at this mess." She offered him a cheery smile as she grabbed several empty cartons and rose. "I better clean up. I really appreciate the meal, Rick. It was fabulous, best date in a bar I've ever had."

She turned to head to the bar. Engrossed, she didn't hear him behind her. His hand gently encircled her upper arm, the weight of it stopping her in her tracks. Slowly he turned her to face him. His eyes, when they met hers, melted into pools of white heat, burning her to the core.

Chapter Eleven

His mouth, only a soft breath from hers, hesitated, his eyes searched her face. Boldly she met his deep brown, almost black gaze, letting slip the curtain that covered the hungry need she felt ripple through her. She nodded almost imperceptibly.

His hand moved to her cheek, stroking her face.

"You are so beautiful." His voice held a wondering note that filled her with need.

She smiled.

Right back at you, Rick Frazier.

His sensual mouth moved over hers, softly at first, the caress whisper light, feathery, questioning. Parting her lips, the flat of his tongue licked over her bottom lip, then nibbled gently at the soft skin there. Urgent need replaced the gentle strokes as his tongue danced over hers in fierce possession. Fire licked her body, moved to center like lava in her groin. Arms wrapped around her to pull her close along the length of his powerful body. She wanted this man, needed to have him eat her alive, fill every inch of her. The passion between them held an electric charge that melted her into helpless pool of want. Styrofoam containers dropped to the floor all around their feet.

Her arms reached around his back and her hands caressed the hard muscles she found there through his T-shirt, then they moved up to wind in his long hair. Her panties dampened with the liquid seeping from her slit. She splayed her legs on either side of one of his rock hard thighs, pressing into him. The action lifted the hem of her skirt to mold her aching cunt against him. She rubbed her pussy over the powerful muscles.

He dragged his mouth from hers. Eyes, heavy and half lidded, assessed her. "You're so incredibly sexy, Becky. You have no idea how much I want you." His thumb and forefinger held her chin in a velvet covered embrace. The thick pad of his thumb moved over her lower lip then dipped erotically into her mouth. After licking the thick digit with the flat of her tongue, he then covered her lower lip with its moisture rubbing over the surface seductively. She sucked his thumb back in with a wicked grin, licking over the surface while he pumped it in and out of her mouth.

"God woman, your mouth is so hot." Her tongue danced around his thumb in promise. His free hand moved down her back to cup a lace covered ass cheek. Strong fingers massaged the globes of her ass while his thumb reminded her of the hard cock that strained between them.

He pulled his thumb from her mouth and pulled her lips to his. Moaning into his mouth, she wriggled against him. His lips traveled to her neck, where they set off uncontrollable tremors wherever his tongue moved against her skin.

"You feel so good, Becky. I want you so much. Let me touch you, play with you, pleasure you, please you."

A sighed response tumbled from her lips almost without thought. She was lost in a fog of sexual need so intense she no longer felt coherent. Her hands fumbled for the button on his jeans. She tugged on the material and pulled them down over his hard ass and powerful legs. Following with her body she squatted before him, putting her at eye level with his massive erection. Long, hard and as thick as promised when it rested against her ass the week before, it thrust proudly between his thighs. Tight balls rested beneath. Licking her lips, she looked up at his face.

"You're huge." It came out as a squeak.

He chuckled, low and throaty. "Not too big I hope." His face turned serious, his voice full of need. "Is this what you want, sweet Becky?" When she nodded, the tension eased from his features. "Please taste me, sweetheart. I want your sexy mouth on me."

His sweet words motivated her lust soaked brain.

She nipped him with her teeth and stroked the flat of her tongue over the head of his engorged member. A pearl of pre-cum dotted the tip, salty on her tongue, wholly masculine and irresistible. The taste fueled her desire, pulling her back for more. Breathing deep, she took in the heady male scent, filled her nostrils with his hot musk. Softly she kissed the purple tip. The thick cock throbbed invitingly in front of her, while above her a sharply indrawn breath from this sexy man turned her eyes lust-filled and unseeing.

One hand grasped the thick base of his cock, the skin of it velvety soft, belying the hardness beneath. Her hand wandered over the flesh, feeling his throbbing need, while the other reached between his legs to lift the weight of his compact balls. Her gaze lifted to his and she leaned in and placed the engorged head in her mouth. Licking over the tip, she sucked furiously, moving her tongue over its mushroom shape. Her hand worked the shaft up and down, squeezing gently, then harder as her hand moved faster.

The smell of his desire mixed with needy moans as she devoured him in long, ice cream cone licks. Hot raw want filed her. She loved the feel of this sexy man fucking her mouth. Felt the naked power of his need wrap around her like a warm blanket on a cold night.

"Shit, Becky, that feels so good. God, sweetheart, suck me, take it all."

With a naughty little smile around the now slick head, she opened her throat and took him to the hilt, savoring his gasped reaction. His hands knotted in her hair, encouraging her to move her mouth further down over his shaft. She responded by licking wildly at the underside of his cock, then she pulled her head back only to plunge down the length of him once more.

The taste and feel of him in her mouth was heaven. Her head bobbed, lips stretched taut as she took in the thick length of him.

"Damn, that's so good. Eat my cock, sweet girl. Watching you suck me is one of the most erotic things I've ever seen."

The head popped out of her mouth, and she stroked the length of him as she looked into his dark eyes. "I want you, Rick. I need you to come in my mouth."

He shuddered as she wrapped her mouth around him once more, slurping the thick head into its depths as far as she could. Sucking his length to the base, she reveled in the feel of his hands fisted tightly in her hair. They held her head steady while he gently fucked her mouth. He shook, signaling his imminent climax. She grasped the base hard to hold off his orgasm and his guttural groans filled her ears. Her mouth pulled free from him once more. "Don't hold back, Rick. Fuck my mouth, take it. I want to make you feel amazing."

She sucked him deep into her in one smooth swallow, pistoning her head up and down on the thick shaft as hard as she could, her rhythm now driven by the thrust of his hips against her lips. While his hands steadied her head, the bunched muscles of his ass drove him into her mouth to the hilt. She groaned in victory as he pumped into her over and over. Yet she knew he was holding back, not fucking her with his full power. Moving her tongue over him, she swallowed still more of the thick member down her throat. Her cheeks hollowed as she placed more sucking pressure on the length of him. Her whole mind focused on devouring the thick monster filling her mouth. Her hands cupped his balls, running damp fingers over the tight feel of them.

Incoherent words fell around her like spring rain, enthralling her. She felt her panties become soaked as she gave in to the moment with wild abandon, a glutton at the table of his lust.

His voice fell out in a croak. "Becky, honey, pull back now or I'm going to come in your mouth." His hands dug almost painfully into her hair. She could feel him trying to pull away from her.

Her eyes flickered up, savoring his struggle not to fill her mouth. She wanted it. She'd never been a girl who swallowed, but this time she wanted her mouth filled with his come. Needed him to lose control, fuck her mouth with abandon.

A wicked smile hovered on her lips. Surrounding his cock she licked down the length in a long powerful stroke. His whole body tightened, seeming to draw in on itself in preparation of his orgasm. Holding her head still, he pumped his thick cock into her mouth while he howled out his release. Moving to the head, she worked the length of him, sucking the last of his come from his balls. She licked his cock clean, dropping a kiss to the tip as she pulled away.

He pulled her to her feet and his mouth consumed hers. Once again his hands roamed her ass. She bunched her skirt to her waist to offer him greater access.

Hissing hot breath filled her ears. "Delicious Becky, I'm going to eat you right up"

Pulling back, she looked into his eyes, then away. "You don't have to do that, Rick. Not what I think you're going to do."

A strong finger caressed her cheek and his gaze locked on hers. "I want to eat your tasty pussy, sweetheart. Don't you want me to?" He sounded slightly wounded, confused.

"Well sure, but the taste..." She shrugged, looking down once again.

His finger gently tilted her face up. He was smiling down at her. "The taste is a sweet one. Let me eat you up. I want to taste you, lick you till you're crying for it. Let me."

She buried her head in his shoulder and nodded, unable to look him in the eye.

The hands embraced her ass once again, lifted her. With a yelp of surprise she wrapped her legs around him, the crotch of her soaked panties pressed hard against the rock-like planes of his stomach.

He sat her on the edge of the nearby stage and then his hands played down over her body. Fitting them to her breasts, the heat from them traveled through her T-shirt and bra, perking her nipples into hard nubs. Flicking his thumbs over them, he pressed against her pussy with his body.

"Do you like that, Becky?"

The heated "yes" felt torn from her throat.

"Tell me what you want me to do to you, baby."

She gasped. "No, please don't make me."

His fingers became rougher, pinching hard, drawing a yelp from her lips. Her pussy was slick wet now. The cream slithered to the crack of her ass, dampening the space under her. Half

100

hysterically, she made a mental note to clean it up later. Surely a puddle this size wouldn't be dry by the time the club opened.

"Say it, Becky, tell me what you need. Do you want me to touch you here with my tongue?" His fingers slipped over her panty-clad pussy, almost stroking her clit through the fabric. They flicked over the depression that denoted the cleft in her labia, teasing her with a gentle touch.

Her hips lifted off the stage floor, pressing her pussy towards his fingers with desperate need.

"Is that what you want, Becky? Tell me you want me to suck that pretty little pussy. Tell me to tongue fuck your slit, baby. Just say the words and it's all yours."

She couldn't say them. She didn't talk like that. Still, his hands touching her wet mound through her panties drove her crazy. Her body fought her mind with the need to form actual words and not guttural noises of want and pleasure. Her body won. The words tore from her lips. "Yes, Rick, please. I want it."

"Want what? You can tell me, sweet, please. I need to hear it."

His voice soothed her fears away. "Yes, Rick, lick me, taste me, please."

He chuckled low in his throat. "With pleasure, sexy woman."

His mouth replaced his finger, nibbling her through the soft cloth. Moving his hands to her hips, he tugged her panties down to her knees, pulled her legs together to lift and rest them on one of his shoulders and slipped her panties over her red leather shoes.

His hands ran the length of her legs then gently pried them apart. Knees bent she hooked her heels over his shoulders. She was completely open and vulnerable to him now. Fighting the urge to bury her face in her hands, she watched him stare at the most intimate part of her.

"You have the most beautiful pussy, Becky. Pink, willing and perfect for my tongue." His finger slid from the bottom of her slit to her clit, teasing the hard bundle of nerves. "Just beautiful," he breathed out.

His hands traveled over the insides of her thighs, stroking her legs from knee to ankle and back. He slipped his finger into her juice covered pussy, then filled her first with one finger, then two, finally adding in a third as he stretched her open for his hungry gaze. He pulled his hand from her and lifted one strong digit to his mouth to lick the juice erotically, tonguing it while she watched fascinated.

"You taste so good to me. Here."

His hand moved almost hypnotically to her mouth, pressing a damp finger lightly to her lips. Opening for him, she tentatively licked his finger in a shy mimicry of his actions.

"See, you don't taste bad, Becky. On the contrary your juicy cunt is delicious."

She shivered at his words and pulled her knees to her shoulders, opening her most private place even further to his lust-filled gaze, wanting to show off her body to him. His words stripped inhibitions from her, left her wanting things she'd never set voice to before. Priming the deep well of her untapped fantasies. Once again his hands moved over her, tantalizingly close to her need. Reaching under her, he sharply grabbed both ass cheeks in his hands lifting her inches off the stage to his waiting hungry mouth.

A wicked low laugh sprang from his lips, pulling cream from her slit. It slipped down the crack of her ass, readying her for his tongue's assault. The first lick drove her hips into his face, nerve endings zinging with the intensity of it. His tongue roving over her pussy and clit drove her to mindlessly writhe on the stage, greedy for more. Her body felt on fire from the ministrations of his tongue.

She'd never had this before, a man buried in her like this, eating her alive. It felt incredibly hot. The fantasy come true exploded through her brain and turned her into a sobbing ball of need before him. Releasing something long bottled and thick within her.

"Do you like that, Becky? Is it good, baby? Do you want me to stop?"

Curling up on her elbows she locked her eyes on his. His lips and chin were wet with her juice. His dark feral eyes held a teasing light. Mouth open, she panted her need to him. Fisting her hands in his hair she pulled him to her weeping pussy once more.

"Suck me, damn you. Make me come."

His smothered laugh of triumph filled her ears with his joy. A warrior replete with won battle.

His big hands squeezed her ass cheeks, opening her completely to his amazing tongue. One hand moved between her legs and a finger entered her, thrust in and out gently at first, then harder. Joined by a second finger his tongue began to lick from his fingers to her hard clit. Biting down gently on her bud drew a tortured moan from her lips. Hips rose to meet his incredible mouth, silently they encouraged him to drive her wild. Sharp teeth nipped gently at fragile nerve endings. Wordless sound flew from her lips, louder and louder. She twisted in frenzied ecstasy against the floor of the stage.

His pumping fingers drove her over the edge. A thick pulse pounded in her ears and the world around her dimmed. She rocketed to orgasm on his nimble tongue, screaming his name in release.

Mind blown, she shuddered against the tongue that lazily licked her. Hands in his hair, she pulled back on his head, seeking relief for the over-sensitized nerve endings. Feeling blasted through her, too much for her brain to absorb. She begged him to stop, but he began a long sensual lick at the base of her slit then moved over her clit to flick furiously against her tortured nerves. Exquisite energy shot through. Head thrown back, mouth open, panting in release, she came once more. Her mind flew to the ceiling in delirium, floating there in a blind haze.

"Shit—Rick, no more. I can't..."

He chuckled. "Okay, sweetheart. That's enough for now."

Lying there, the world around her began to slowly come into focus. The shiny black painted stage, the deep red curtains that hung on either side and the lights suspended like weighted snowflakes from the ceiling. Her universe sharpened and coalesced as she floated back to earth. Lastly, she registered the man whose face was still between her parted thighs.

"Was it good for you?" He was smiling, but behind his deep eyes was a hungry little boy need that charmed her.

The skin of his face, where her hand stroked him, was almost smooth, only a sparse dusting of rough shadow abraded her hand. "I think my toes are permanently damaged from curling. Yes, Rick, it was good for me."

Strong arms pulled his body onto the stage and drew her close. Pillowed against one hard shoulder, his strong unrelenting heartbeat filled her ear. She felt calm, relaxed and safe.

"Mmm, this feels nice." She was purring, actually making a sound like a contented kitten. She'd find it funny if she wasn't so damn satisfied.

His hands roamed her back and his fingers played in her hair, stroking gently. "This feels so amazing, Becky." A kiss landed on the top of her head. "It's almost like you've bewitched me."

Her breath stopped as she took in his statement, rolled the implications around in her brain. Bewitched, enchanted, called to her. Conjured from the desert air in the dead of night. Enslaved. Was that what this was? This man in her arms, the one that had just brought her to mind shattering orgasm, had he been drawn to her with no will of his own? Was this how she'd imagined it? What she'd wanted? A man attracted to her by magic alone. Shit, what was she going to do? Blindly she grabbed the small silver heart nestled between her breasts.

"You know what, Rick? I completely forgot, but I have to be somewhere at eight this morning and I need to run. I'm sorry." She was fighting to keep her voice even, the tone normal.

Feeling her heart thud in her chest, she pulled away from him. She dangled her feet off the stage to hop down. She felt him grab her arm, but his touch seemed far off. All she wanted to do was hide in a quiet place and process her feelings. Just get the hell out of here as fast as possible.

"Becky?" His tone registered confusion, and more than a little hurt.

"No really. I'm sorry," she said, kissing him on the cheek. "I had a great time, Rick. Thanks for dinner. Can you lock up for me?"

She was babbling. Just rattling off anything to hide the fear gnawing at her bowels and ripping her apart.

Dropping to the floor, she dug around for her carelessly tossed panties. Spying the scrap of fabric under a chair, she stood and jammed them into her pocket. Pulling desperately at the hem of her skirt, she yanked it back into place in one jerking motion. Her keys were in her purse. She just had to get to the office. It would be easy to get out the door once she was there.

"Becky, I don't understand. Is everything okay?" Concern laced his voice. The soft tone only made her want to get out of there faster.

"I'm fine. I just forgot that damn appointment." She was halfway to the office now, almost home free.

"Okay. Becky, but are you going to be all right getting home?"

She nodded furiously. Her hand reached around the door where she quickly located her purse by feel. Grabbing it up haphazardly in nerveless fingers, it slipped, dropping to the floor with a smack. Contents spilled out and rolled in all directions.

"Oh shit."

Stupidly, she stood there, just staring down at her favorite lipstick busily rolling out of reach. Her wallet fell open to reveal her drivers license photo. There it lay, a picture of the world's most desperate woman. Tears clogged her throat as she looked up blankly into Rick's concerned brown eyes.

His arms came around her and held her tight to his warm body. The comfort he offered was so tempting. But she was a liar and a fake. He wasn't attracted to her for Becky, just a stupid spell. Leaning into him would be easy, too easy. For a moment she smelled the clean scent of him. The soap and sweat mixed with the musk of sexual release enveloped her in safe warmth. Just a moment, then she reluctantly pulled away.

"I've got to go, Rick," she whispered. "I'm sorry. I can't explain."

"Okay, Becky, I trust you. I'm here if you need me." Bending down he gathered her things into his hands. He fumbled with her lipsticks, his long sexy hair covering his back and shoulders in a black waterfall. Silently he placed the items back in her bag and handed the red leather to her, his eyes pleading.

Taking it from him with a nod, she forced herself to turn away and walked to the door and out into the cold desert night.

Chapter Twelve

"Hey, scrawny, you need a spot?"

Concentration beaded his brow with sweat as Rick hefted the heavy weight towards the sky. He couldn't spare a glance to see who spoke to him, a grunt sufficed for a "yes". Hands joined his as the mass lowered towards his chest. With a groan he pushed it skyward once again. Five reps later, his chest heaving, arms muscles burning like fire, he stopped at the midpoint and hooked the barbell safely in place with a metallic clang.

Sitting up, he wiped the sweat from his eyes with a towel, only to see the gigantic form of Muscles swim into focus.

"Thanks, man. I really needed that spot." Rick grinned at the Goliath. No one had ever called him scrawny before. He'd been working out most of his adult life, but he had nothing on Muscles. Rick stood and wiped down the bench, offering the big man a turn.

He appeared to consider the weights for a moment before he purposefully headed to the display of racked and numbered disks. He grabbed two forty pounders like they were fives and stacked the weights on either end, then moved the collars back into place to ensure the heavy plates would not slide off. "No problem, Rick. Never seen you here before. You a new member?"

"Yeah, courtesy of the Buckin' Bronco. With the group discount and my tips for the last week, I was finally able to join a real gym. The one in my apartment building wasn't cutting it anymore. You need a spot?"

One eyebrow rose almost imperceptibly as the other man looked at Rick with a wry grin. "Spotters? I don't need no steenkin' spotters." He laughed. "Seriously, I do, but its fun to act all macho. Half the guys in here are scared to spot me because of the weight I push."

Rick eyed the stacks on either end of the barbell dubiously. "Um yeah, I can see why that might be. How much you got on there?"

"About three forty or so. It's not that much." The big lug almost looked modest.

Rick burst out laughing. "Yeah right, and I'm the Easter Bunny."

Lying down on the bench and positioning his hands with care, Muscles started humming, "Here Comes Peter Cottontail" as he began to slowly hoist the weight.

Rick positioned his own hands to help in case the other man had an issue at the end of the set. Truthfully, there was no way Rick could heft that mass. His smaller frame maxed out somewhere around two twenty. The whole thing would be a wash if Muscles lost control of the heavy bar.

Watching for a telltale wobble on either end of the barbell, Rick adjusted his stance. Even someone the size of Muscles should be having trouble now, but the big man just kept on for thirteen complete reps. Like a robot, he made each extension of the cumbersome weight look almost easier than the last. It was beautiful, absent the smell of sweat and groans of pain. Reracking the weights, Muscles sat up, his barrel chest blowing breath like a bellows stoking a white hot fire.

"That felt great. You should increase your weight, man." Rick could not mistake the challenging gleam in the bouncer's eyes.

"No thanks, Muscles. I think I'll stick to chicken shit poundage. You about done here?"

He snorted. "Why? You wanna take me out for a smoothie?"

Laughing, Rick returned his hands to the bar in front of him as Hulk-man leaned back into the bench and prepared to push another set. "Gee, Muscles, are you asking me out on a date?"

Grunting around the heavy load, he grinned, his next words punctuating most every lift. "My-wife-might-have-something-to-say-about-that. Oof. Done." He re-racked the weight and sat up. "No really, Frazier, I got some time on my hands. Feel like a run?"

Rick eyed the older, larger man in disbelief. Most muscle heads didn't do a lot of running. Maybe Rick couldn't out lift Muscles, but outrunning him would be a snap. "Sure."

ಸಿ ಉ

The man was a machine. An evil machine that masticated Rick's body and puked him out over the baked Las Vegas dirt in a colorful arch. That was the only way to explain the super fast four mile run they'd just completed. Rick normally ran at a good clip, but Muscles out-performed him in every way.

Butt kissing the curb, head between his knees, Rick gulped lungfuls of air. He was not going to vomit in front of this guy. He had a feeling that bit of news would be all over the bar in about an hour and he'd never live it down. As it was, he just bet that the main topic of conversation among the staff tonight would be Rick's shitty performance at the gym.

Clapping him on the back hard, Muscles shot him a nasty smirk. "Suck it up, buddy. Most guys can't keep up with me. Only Becky gives me a good run for my money. She can even outdo me on the swim."

Straightening, Rick groaned. "You mean you swim, too?"

Stretching out his legs, the behemoth adopted a shit-eating grin. "Yep, and bike. Becky and I race in triathlons together. She didn't mention that to you?"

"Nope, I think I would have remembered something like that. You any good?"

"Me? Nah. I just do it for fun, but Becky places pretty high in her age-group. That's an accomplishment because the competition's pretty tight for women in their early thirties."

"Wait, you mean like that Ironman stuff I see on TV, where first you swim in an ocean full of sharks, then bike in the baking sun for over a hundred miles and finally run a marathon in the middle of the night?"

The shaggy head shook. "Nope, not that long. Maybe for me one day, just as long as it doesn't include an ocean swim, I prefer lakes, but Becky's just out there for the short distances. We do sprints and not in the ocean. I have a jelly-fish issue. You should ask her about it sometime. You spend enough time together." He took a long thoughtful pull from his bottle of water. "So, what's up with that? You got a thing for the boss lady?" He sat on the curb in a way that gave Rick the feeling this was going to be a long chat. Maybe befriending the giant wasn't such a smart idea after all.

"I don't know," Rick studied his shoes. "I thought we had something started, but she slipped out on me. I'm not sure it's gonna happen. Have you known her long?"

Opening a new bottle of water the bouncer dumped the contents over his head. "Ahh, refreshing." He shook his shaggy head playfully, spaying Rick with a mixture of water and sweaty drops. "Let's see... I met her when I first came to work at the bar ten years ago. She'd come out to visit her grandma on long weekends and school breaks, help out at the bar. She was a good kid. Sure does love the old lady. I was happy when she took over the place. Lucy's a great gal, but she's also an ornery old pain-in-the-ass. Becky's a lot steadier. The guys really like working for her."

Rick swallowed hard. "Does she date a lot of guys from the bar?"

Again, Muscles shook his head. "Nope, never seen her even show an interest in the guys before you. When she was in school, she'd hole up in that nightmare of an office with her books. After that, she was busy climbing the corporate ladder. I don't think she'd let herself fall for a guy." He cocked his brow at Rick. "You do know the person you should be talking to about this shit is Becky, right?"

"Hey, you brought it up." Rick's sigh sounded too long and damn irritated, even to him. "Yeah, I know. She just took off on me last night, though. Up and ran off mid-sentence. I don't have a clue what I said to her."

Standing, Muscles let out a barking laugh. "Who the hell knows with women? I don't understand my wife at all. She's one nutty broad, but she makes my clock tick, if you get my meaning. Speaking of the old lady, I'd better head home. She'll kick my ass if I'm late."

Rick rose and looked at the colossal giant dubiously. "I better let you go then. Since you're whipped and all." He smiled jokingly.

"Yeah, well better whipped and happy than proud and lonely. Speaking of whipped, you gonna be back here tomorrow?"

Rick chuckled at the snarky look on the older man's face. "Sure, I love abuse. Bring it on."

"Good, maybe I'll get you on a bike for a nice twenty miler into the desert. I'll be here 'bout two if you're interested."

With that he trotted off across the street and back into the club, leaving Rick shaking his head. His whole body was going to hurt like hell tomorrow. Too bad his damn male pride would make sure his sore ass was back here promptly at two the next day.

Later he headed into the locker room to shower his soon to be aching body and re-played the conversation with Muscles. The man had some good points. It seemed that whatever else was going on in her head, Becky had some genuine feelings for him. Interesting, damned interesting.

He changed into his street clothes and headed to his car, figuring it was time to come to a decision about Becky Blake. He didn't have a clue what was up with the adorably curvaceous strip club owner, but he wasn't about to give up on her. She had something. Something that made him hot and bothered...and it was more than her delicious body. She had a way of washing his hurts clean and replacing them with hope.

Sliding into the hot car, he felt his leg muscles cramp all along their length. Damn, Muscles had been brutal. A trip to a drug store was in order. There was no way in hell he was going into work limping like an old man in front of Becky and the guys. The exercise robot wasn't getting the better of Rick Frazier.

The ringing of his cell phone interrupted his thoughts. Turning the car's air-conditioner to high, he reached into his gym bag and glanced at the display. Shit, it was Tara again. Why did he have to be one of those people who felt obligated to answer a ringing phone? Right now he admired people who could just ignore the damn things.

Turning the vents full on his face, he pushed the talk button. "Hey Tara, what's up?"

"Is that any way to greet your wife?" She was practically purring, typical Tara. She was up to something, she always sounded like a cat in heat when she was about to manipulate him.

"Ex-wife, Tara. We're no longer married." He tried to keep his voice even, the impatience on a tight leash.

"Well you're the one that filed for divorce. Not me."

He could practically hear her pout through the phone.

"I didn't really have a choice, if you'll accurately remember the circumstances. I have to go to work now. What do you want, Tara?" The car finally felt cold. His tight muscles relaxed a bit in the chill.

"Ouch, you're a grump today. I need to talk to you."

"So talk, I have a little time. A very little."

"No, Rick, I need to see you in person. Can you fly out and visit me?"

"No, Tara, I can't. I have to work. If you need to talk please do it in a phone call."

"Please, Rick. I wouldn't ask, but it's real important. It's just a stupid bartending job. Your real work won't suffer." She was pleading again, and seemed on the verge of tears. This sure didn't sound like her usual game. The one thing he knew for certain about Tara was she had a plan for getting things out of him. A stair step escalation that never varied, never wavered. She'd skipped three whole steps. This must be important.

"Look, I can't, Tara," he apologized. "I have to work. Right now that bartending job is paying both our bills." He sighed, letting the air out in a slow hiss between his teeth. "If you have to see me that bad you can come here."

"Great! I've always wanted to see Vegas. You can show me around and take me out. It'll be just like old times." He could hear the brightening in her voice, the smile she gave whenever she won an argument or got her way.

"Tara, you're welcome to come to talk to me, but it's going to have to be a quick visit. I have a project I'm hoping to sell, not to mention my work. I don't have time to show you all over town." What the hell was she up to? Didn't the word "divorce" mean anything to this woman?

"Oh, you'll work it all out," she said breezily. "I just know we'll have a blast together." Her voice lowered huskily. "I miss you, baby."

"Yeah, great, Tara. I have to go. Just leave me a message with your flight information and I'll pick you up at McCarran."

Clicking the "end call" button, he stared at the steering wheel as if it would speak to him, telling him what his devious ex was up to. He'd ask himself what he'd ever seen in her, but he knew. She'd been so different from the girls he grew up with, who were all dark, short and curvy. Tara epitomized leggy blonde elegance. Her hollow cheeks and arresting blue eyes promised him a world beyond the poverty of the Rez. She'd made no secret of her interest in him from the moment they'd met.

She'd enthralled him. Her suburban practicality had bordered on the glamorous in his rural born and bred eyes. It had been a two-way street. Tara was what the guys on the Rez called a, "Brave Collector". He'd seen them all his life, people that came to the Reservation to look at "Indians" like animals in a zoo. All his friends laughed about it. Many of them took advantage of what the young women so eagerly offered. Rick had scoffed at them, claimed he'd never fall for one of the giggling girls who thought fry-bread was alien food. Then college had beckoned.

Feeling out of place and homesick, it had been far too easy to fall for someone like Tara. Bubbly and fun to be around, she enchanted him with her willing body and pretty looks. Marrying her had been all hormones and starry-eyed romance. Her parents hated Rick, had called him a "dirty Indian" to his face. When they'd forced Tara to choose between them, Rick had proposed on the top of a mountain. Running off together to start a new life in San Francisco seemed so glamorous. Working with his college buddy...a dream come true. The business took off, grew bigger than any of them could believe. His life had felt like a fantasy. Until it all came crashing down the day he'd come home early.

Rick had never thought that Tara was attracted to him for his ancestry until he'd found the two of them together. Not even bothering to dress, she'd started berating him, screaming out her poison while Rick stood there numb. One of the pissy crap-ass reasons she'd flung at him as he'd packed his things in silence, was that Rick was not a "real Indian". Apparently his half white background had been offensive to her, while his partner's African American heritage turned her on. She found him far more exotic and appealing.

Bitter some? Time to go to work.

Thoughts of his employment brought a smile to his lips. Becky was the antithesis of Tara. He needed her. Not only was she adorable, smart and sexy as hell, she just might be the one thing between a life of happiness or becoming a bitter twisted old man full of unfulfilled dreams. Smiling wryly, he turned the key in the ignition and pulled out of the parking lot. Time to see his delectable boss.

Chapter Thirteen

"Hey, Becky, you're boobs are showing." What felt like three hundred pairs of eyes turned to stare at her cleavage. Self consciously, she snapped the mother of pearl button closed for the third time tonight.

"Cute, Tom. Next time could you maybe yell it a bit louder so everyone in the place can hear?"

The dress had been her grandmother's. Pure vintage 70's western-type wear, it fit like a glove, especially in the ta-ta area. The red checked gingham made her feel like a tablecloth with boobs, but it was the only thing she'd had in the closet clean and ready to wear to work. The short, three-tiered skirt barely covered her hind end when she bent over. Perky capped sleeves finished the look. She always felt almost naked in this dress, but the clients loved it. Told her she looked like a, "Cute little cowgirl".

Yippee ki yi yay.

The top was a shade too tight and she always ended up re-snapping the thing at least five times a night. Finally, she'd given in to the dratted dress and paired it with a red lacy push up bra so if anything popped out, at least it matched. This outfit was racier than the jeans and tight black T's she normally wore, but after years of things remaining the same, any change was a welcome change.

Cut the crap, Beckers, you wore this for Rick.

She smiled. It was true. She felt horrible about the night before. The combination of his innocent words, her fear of relationships in general, along with the raw uninhibited nature of their sex scared the poo right out of her.

She'd never been with anyone so totally male in her life. His body had been incredible sure, but more than that, the connection they seemed to share had been magnetic.

She'd been a heel. A big ole red high heel of a heel. An apology was certainly in order and she'd be happy to give him one. Just as soon as she screwed up her courage she'd march right up to him and say, "Hey, Rick, I should have stuck around longer for the pillow talk last night, but I cast this spell and when you said I'd bewitched you, well then naturally..." Blah, blah, blah. Oh yeah, that sounded like a fabulous idea. Maybe in a week or so when she was stronger. The problem with that boneheaded plan was that it was Saturday night and the boys behind the bar were getting slammed as usual. Pretty soon she was going to have to stop wandering the room and greeting the guests and go back there to help the poor suckers out.

Gird your loin's, girl, and march your behind right into Rick land.

She made it sound like he was an amusement ride.

Well the man is one hell of a sexual rollercoaster.

The D-jay announced Tom, who slinked onto the stage dressed as a naughty cop. This was one of the Buckin' Bronco's most popular acts. Some poor woman, usually a bride or birthday girl, was handcuffed to the pole on the stage while Tom danced and rubbed his body over his victim of the day. Always to the woman's and the audience's delight. Apparently admiring the stripper was thirsty work for the masses of screaming ladies who swarmed the stage. His dance always resulted in a rush at the bar, the customers cooling their fueled blood with fresh ice cold beverages.

No more avoiding the cute bartender. Into the fray, Becky.

She rounded the bar only to be met with Rick's welcoming smile. He seemed genuinely glad to see her, the corners of his eyes displaying fine lines. She didn't know if this made the whole guilt over last night thing worse or not. It was hard to face him either way, that was for sure. This man was the hottest thing since sliced bread and he seemed to be into her. Or...or it was the result of a spell and she'd messed with his free will. Did he find her attractive or...was it the magic?

"Hey, Becky, it's nice to see you."

"For my amazing bartending ability?" She smiled, trying to convey the joke, but he looked at her oddly. She never could crack a decent joke.

"No, I meant that. I'm glad to see you."

"Oh." Dropping her chin, she grabbed a long neck from the open-topped cooler in front of her. She twisted it open and placed it on the bar in one smooth practiced motion, plopping it in front of a startled patron.

"Miss, I'm sorry, I didn't order this," the woman said apologetically.

Becky looked up, embarrassed. "It's on the house, enjoy."

"Thanks." The appreciative patron grabbed the beer and dropped a buck in its place.

Scooping up the dollar, Becky dumped it, with more force than necessary, into the communal tip jar. Her face flamed. She could not spend the rest of her life being so scatterbrained. She glanced down and a discarded slice of orange caught her eye. The action of bending over to pick up the wayward fruit slice stuck her ass out, right into Rick's tight jean-covered cock. The member pressed with sexy familiarity into her thong-covered backside. She yelped as the contact sent electric heat right through her body to center on her pussy. Feeling liquid begin to dampen her crotch, she shot up. Whap! Her head came into star-seeing contact with the overhang of the bar.

"Oh shit, Becky, are you okay, sweetheart?" The concern in his voice, while gratifying, seemed to be coming from very far off.

One hand on her aching head, she reached out the other to the edge of the bar to steady herself while she tried to stand again, this time with more care. The world wobbled around her as Rick's arm shot out to capture her elbow, guiding her.

"Okay, obviously not. Tad, can you handle it for a bit? I'm going to get her back to the office."

"Sure 'nuff."

She giggled almost hysterically at his response. No one had ever accused Tad of being verbose. *Ouch.* The pain that shot through her brain seemed to connect with her eyes, blurring the world around her to an out of focus picture. Nausea swept over her, causing her to almost bend double in agony.

She felt Rick's hand on her arm, his concern apparent in the gentle way he directed her to the tacky back room.

Gratefully, she sank down onto the pink leather couch. Her head pounded like something or someone was trying to dig its way out through her eyeballs.

"Becky, sweetheart, can you look at me?"

His voice still sounded like it came from the bottom of a well. Lifting her eyes to his, she blinked several times.

Coming to his feet, he flipped the light switch, closing the door at the same time. Pain shot through her nerve endings, as her brain fuzzled in an attempt to adjust her eyes to the change in illumination. She had one monster headache and that damned light was not helping.

Her arm lifted to shield her eyes. "Damn, Rick, that's bright."

"Sorry, sweetheart. I have to look at your pupils to see if you have a concussion. You can do it here or at the ER, your choice."

She giggled, then winced, this really hurt. She had to remember to keep from laughing. No amount of funny was worth this torment. "Are you a doctor, too? That is on top of software creator and bartender par excellence?"

His teeth flashed white as he smiled at her. "Nope, but on the reservation, doctors are not always close by and emergency rooms are few and far between. You learn how to judge a situation from a young age. Plus, my mom taught first aid classes for the Red Cross to make some extra money. She made me tag along to keep me out of trouble. Got a flashlight?"

She indicated a desk drawer with a sweep of her hand. He didn't even have to stand to reach it. He just leaned over her and pulled it open to retrieve the light, then turned back to her.

"Here we go."

Light flashed in each of her eyes in turn. The brilliance forced her head back.

"Sorry about the bright light in your eyes. I have to do it though. Now follow my finger." His manner soothed her. Her eyes followed the index finger he held up as he slowly traced it back and forth, up and down. "Excellent, Becky. I don't think you have a concussion, but I'm going to watch you for a bit.

She nodded, yawning, the quiet of the office making her suddenly sleepy.

"You look beat. You wanna lie down for a while?"

"I should get back to the bar, Rick. It's busy out there."

He craned his head to peek out the two-way glass and assess the action at the bar. "It's not that busy, Becky, it looks like it might even be starting to wind down. Tad and the guys have it under control. You can take a short nap. Do you need some Ibuprofen?"

"Probably, I have some stuff in the top drawer there."

She watched him pull out the familiar red and white bottle, then hand her two small pills. Popping them into her mouth, she swallowed without water.

A whistle of appreciation signaled his approval. "Wow, that's impressive."

She grinned. "I went to college. Hangovers R Us U."

"You were a party animal? You're kidding me." His teasing brown eyes were deep enough to fall into. So dark she wasn't sure where the pupils ended and the rich chocolate of his irises began.

"Only on the weekends. The rest of the time I was a good girl with my head buried in a book."

"Here, move over." He joined her on the couch, then gently coaxed her head down to lie on his lap. Cripes, he wanted her to rest? How was she supposed to manage that with her head resting against his crotch? Her head pillowed on his powerful thighs sent her libido into over drive. Her blood sang in her veins.

Before she could get too torqued up, his strong hands began to caress her hair. Soothing over it and down its length. Tingles raced over her scalp and soft lights of pleasure swirled in her brain. The calming feeling of his touch relaxed her. She felt a third yawn overcome her.

"That feels wonderful, Rick. Don't stop." She snuggled deeper into the welcome warmth of his lap.

His hands stilled, then started their delicious distraction once more. "I know this isn't an ideal time, what with your head injury and all, but I was sort of hoping to talk to you about last night."

Her eyes popped open and her head lifted off his lap several inches, bringing renewed pain as she turned to face him, heart pounding in her chest.

'Um...well I'm not sure I'm ready to talk about that quite yet." *Maybe never.*

"Shhh. I didn't say you had to talk. It's my turn. You just have to lie there and listen. Deal?"

Reluctantly her head returned to his lap. She put a hand to her mouth to cover her shyness. Her muffled, "I guess," floated up around her as she hid, once more, in his exquisitely powerful thighs.

His fingers resumed their slow caress of her hair. The combination of the comforting touch and his soft voice lulled her into a magical space of comfort. Nothing felt like it could hurt her here, in his arms.

"I've been thinking about the way things ended last night."

"Uh huh."

"Shhh."

Willing herself to lie still and listen, she bit her lip.

"I don't know why you need time, Becky, and I don't need to know. I just want you to understand that you have it. It's all in your hands now. We can take this as slow and easy as you want. Whatever you need. You call the shots. I just want to see more of you."

Laughter rumbled from him. "But please don't wait too long or I think my cock might explode. Because, sweet Becky, I want to make love to you. Just as soon as you let me, I'm going to bend you over and fuck you till you're screaming my name."

She knew her panties were wet, soaked in fact, could feel the liquid pearl over her mound. She was probably leaving a damp spot on the couch as the juice flowed around her thong and out the bottom of her short skirt. What was it young teenage boys said about girls? "Snail trails?" Yep, that was an apt description.

"I don't know what to say, Rick."

"You don't have to say anything. Just think about it. Picture our coming together in your mind. You already know how intense it will be."

She did. Deep in the core of her she knew that last night had nothing on what they could be together. Still, the spell... Were these his words? Or were they being pulled from him unknowingly by the magic she'd created on a cold night? She bit her lip.

His fingers moved to massage her sore neck muscles, pulling the tension from her with an expert touch. Turning her face deeper into his lap to better enjoy the calming treatment, she sighed. This was nice, very nice. The world, her worries and a bar full of screaming women melted under this man's careful ministrations. She relaxed completely into his hard sexy lap, feeling herself slip into sleep.

Chapter Fourteen

Warm fuzziness surrounded her. Burrowing deeper under the blanket, she fought against the annoying tickle in her brain that told her something was not quite right. Damn, it was no good. Sleep slipped from her, receded to a pinpoint and winked out. She opened her eyes. It was dark in her office, not quite pitch, but still pretty tomblike. She sat up and looked out the two-way into the bar. The red exit sign eternally glowed above the doors, but other than that the bar was empty and dark. What time was it? Head turning, she scanned the inky black for the illuminated face of the clock on her desk.

Her sleepy brain tried to make sense of the numbers. Three thirty? That couldn't possibly be right. That would mean she'd slept through close. The long hours she'd kept must have finally gotten to her.

The cozy nest on the couch suddenly seemed cloying, and her eyelids felt thick and gritty. She pushed the covers off and padded on bare feet to investigate the bar, hitting the light switch with a fingertip as she passed. The countertop gleamed, glasses sat racked and ready for the night to come and every chair was a sentinel atop sparkling clean tables. Moving to the front door, she pulled twice. Locked tight. All in order. Tad was an outstanding bartender, but he always managed to miss a few things in the clean up. This had to be Rick's doing. She smiled.

Her head felt a lot better now, pretty darn near normal. Her tongue rolled around her mouth, exploring the sandpaper taste. She was dry. Moving to the gleaming oak bar, she pulled down a glass and drew a beer.

It wasn't often she indulged in a drink after work. Most nights she was just so damned tired to do anything but drive right home and crash fully clothed onto her bed. It vaguely occurred to her that drinking alcohol after a head injury was not the smartest idea known to man, but lately she'd been awash in dumb shit ideas. What was one more?

She plopped her hind end on the barstool and slid back, swinging her feet as she sipped the ice cold beer. The silence of the place almost overwhelmed her as her mind spun into uncomfortable Rick territory. Ugh, she didn't want to go there right now. She was damned tired of the stress of not knowing whether this was the work of honest sexual chemistry, or the spell, that drove their relationship. She chugged back a healthy swallow of the amber colored liquid, hitched her feet over the brass footrest, and leaned in to pour herself another one.

Delicious

It was still too quiet. She needed some music to make her alone time perfect. She hopped off the stool, careful not to spill any of the amber liquid on the clean floors. She made a determined beeline for the D-jay booth that sat on one corner of the stage.

She hit the master control switch on the lights, then the small lamp over the booth. The CD's, stacked in a neat pile, called to her and she began to paw through the mixes. Most were labeled for specific strippers, while the rest were just a generic collection to entertain between sets when the guys went into the crowd for tabletop dances. Pulling out one of her favorites, "Strippers Mix", she then popped it in the player.

Aerosmith's, "Love in an Elevator" filled the bar, blasting in an almost physical wave over her body. She hit the sliding control for the stage lights, bringing them up to full.

Electric energy filled her and she danced behind the booth, spinning wildly in a circle while holding her now almost empty beer tight. Her hair arched behind her then brushed her shoulders as she stopped to change directions. Carefully, she placed the beer on the drink stand next to the booth as the music shifted to, "Just Push Play". Her hips slipped to the beat, circling tightly under her as she moved to the center of the stage.

She dropped to her knees, hands sliding up her torso to mold and squeeze her breasts. Her head flipped forward. Long hair covered her face as she peeped from behind it into the blaze of the lights.

She flipped her hair back and reached behind her to lift the shining mass off her neck, then she let it fall around her in soft swirls. Her hand moved to her lips and she played there a moment before one finger sucked into her mouth. Releasing the digit, she snaked it down, leaving a wet trail leading to the top snap of her dress. She toyed with the mother of pearl before pulling the fastener apart, a hint of her red lace bra now on display to the empty audience. A second finger joined the first and another snap parted to reveal her cleavage. Two snaps now undone, her hands circled her breasts, lifting them up as she pouted her lips and offered her mounds to the invisible audience.

Breasts cradled in her hands, she pinched and pulled the nipples through the fabric. Then she stood, gathered the skirt of her dress up, and turned to display her thong-covered ass to the up-ended chairs. In her imagination she danced for Rick, turning him on, making him hard. She saw his body ready for her, his eyes smoldering with need. She turned to once again face the imaginary audience of one. Her hands moved back to the open front of her dress and she ripped apart the remaining snaps in one smooth, savage move. The dress slipped from one, then the other of her shoulders. With a kittenish glance into the empty seats, she stripped the rest of the dress away, and with casual disdain, tossed it to the stage behind her.

Naked, save for her bra and thong panties, she ran to the pole, grabbed as high as she could and flew through the air expertly. Her body wound sinuously down its length, ending in the splits at the bottom.

Chapter Fifteen

Holy shit. Scratch that. Holy fucking shit! His hands moved to his eyes to rub away the remnants of sleep. He needed to be sure the image his brain processed was really there. Yep, Becky still rode the pole, spinning like a top to the throbbing beat of heavy metal. Hot damn, she looked amazing. Where the hell had she learned to strip like that? He'd almost come in his jeans when she'd ripped her dress off her tight curvy body. Now she was a goddess in sinful red, long hair flying behind her, a feral half-aware look on her beautiful face.

He had the vague notion that he should return to the couch in the dressing room. Just slip quietly back to sleep and stop invading her privacy. Clearly she had no idea he'd slept there to keep an eye on her. He doubted she'd be dancing almost nude if she knew he ogled her, a voyeur in the dark bar. Maybe he should cough, let on that he was standing not five feet from the stage, staring at one of her nipples as it escaped the confines of her bra? Screw it. Watching her dance so provocatively mesmerized him. He couldn't speak if his life depended on it, let alone suck in enough air in to cough.

She dropped to her hands and knees, all stalking animal and sex as she clawed her way across the stage. Her tight body showed off sleek muscle beneath tanned skin. Her breasts, full and high under the lace of her bra, begged to be freed. Damn, his cock was hard. If she took off that bra he was done for.

Laying, back she V'd her legs in the air, giving him a glorious display of bunched muscle filled out with soft curves. She pulled her legs beneath her and, rising gracefully, danced to the pole once again. While her legs wrapped around the shining length like a pro, he envisioned them encircling his body. He'd made her promises. Meant every word of them. But right now, sitting on the edge of a table not far from the stage, his cock filling out the front of sweats, he questioned every damn one of them. He was in pain and not sure how much more he could take of this sweet torment. She moved from the pole just as the music changed to a slower beat. Slinking to the middle of the stage, she then fell to the floor in the splits. Cripes he was going to be undone by this hot little vixen.

Sinuously, she rolled to her stomach, then pushed up to rest on her knees. Her small hands trailed up her body, starting with her thighs and heading up to the lace of her panties. The look in her eyes was hot enough to set the stage curtains on fire as she toyed with the elastic. Lips curved into a devil's smile, her hands reached behind her back. A shimmy of her shoulders and her bra straps slipped down as she molded the cups of the garment to her playfully. Turning her back to the bar, she let the bra fall forward and then tossed it into the air behind her. The red lace and satin landed smack in Rick's hands.

Did she know he was there? Could she feel his presence in the room? No, the stage lights prevented anyone from seeing into the audience more than a few feet. She had no clue what she was doing to him, how hard she'd made his cock. How much he wanted to thrust it into her aching cunt over and over again.

That she was unaware she had an audience made her show all the hotter. Bending over once more, her thumbs hooked the elastic sides of her thong. Exposing her ass, she pulled them down her legs in one smooth motion. Her nether lips were now visible at the apex of her thighs. A glorious pink pouting display. He'd not had time to admire her pretty bare pussy the night before, now he looked his fill at the puffy lips. God, was it only last night that he'd had her dripping her sweet juices over his tongue? It felt a million years ago.

Standing, she turned to face him again. Her fingers pinched her pert nipples as she tossed her head back in seeming ecstasy. She rotated, her movement's fluid and sensual as she slid her arms around the pole. Her back to it, he imagined her ass cheeks as they must look nestled against the hard smooth surface between them. Her body slipped down its length until she was squatting, heels together, legs open to his lust filled eyes. She licked the tip of one finger, her tongue playing over the surface, then slid the length into her mouth, her lips pursing as she sucked. Down her body it traveled, one tantalizing inch at a time until it rested above her delicious little clit, then rubbed over it as her mouth formed in a needy "O".

Rick's hand moved to the front of his sweats. He intended to just shift his cock to make it more comfortable, but his rebellious hand stroked it several times through the soft fabric as he watched her touch herself. His member ached and his mouth watered at the self-inflicted assault on her damp pink flesh.

He must have made some small sound, groaned his desire loud enough to be heard over the music, because her slender fingers stilled and her eyes widened. Blindly, she searched the bright wash of light for the source of the noise.

"Is there someone there?"

There was fear in her voice. He thought about sneaking out, pretending he'd never been there, but that would have been cruel. Standing up now, she reached for her dress and shielded her gorgeous body from his view.

"Hello? Is anybody there?" This time a note of panic crept in at the end of her sentence.

He was caught. The best course of action was to speak up. Tell her he was there and allay her fears.

"Sorry, Becky, it's just me. I didn't mean to scare you, sweetheart."

"Rick? Is that you?" He could be wrong, but he could swear he heard hope in her tone.

He shouted to be heard clearly over the music. "Yeah, it's me." The, "me" echoed loudly in the stillness as she shut the tune off.

She blushed furiously. He caught the embarrassed look on her face as her hand reached for the master light board behind the D-jay stand. With a flip of her fingers, the stage plunged into almost total darkness, the light behind the bar now the only illumination. His eyes fought to adjust to the dark. He couldn't see her and he wanted to, needed to...see her face. Know what she felt. He didn't want to scare her, just the opposite.

"Umm, Rick?" Her tentative words floated to him out of the darkness.

"What, sweetheart?"

She giggled. "I can't find my bra."

The laughter behind the statement reassured him. She wasn't dying of embarrassment. Relief flooded over him in a heady wash.

"Well, if you hadn't turned the light off you wouldn't be having this problem now, would you, little lady?"

"What, and let you see me turn the color of my dress? I don't think so."

Approaching the stage and careful to avoid the tables, he listened as the sound of her voice dropped lower. Presumably the woman was crawling around on the stage in search of the missing article of clothing. He felt almost guilty about the scrap of red lace draped over his fingers, almost... He grinned.

"You're looking in the wrong spot." He could make her form out in the low light now. Watched her still as she absorbed his words.

"I gather you have information that could lead to its safe return?"

"I do."

She laughed. "I take it there's some sort of ransom involved here?"

"There is."

"I don't suppose you'd care to share the price with me?"

"Oh, I expect you'll find out if you come over here."

"Rick?"

"Yeah, sweetie?"

"I'm scared." Her voice was filled with hesitant need.

"Why?"

She moved to the edge of the stage. "If I have sex with you I'm going to be lost." He barely heard the whispered words.

He drew in a wobbly breath. His reached out in the darkness, encountering the sleek fall of her hair. "I already am, Becky Blake. Already lost in those incredible understanding eyes of yours, the smell of your skin, the feel of you against me. Your warm heart. I became lost in you the first time I laid eyes on you."

In the thick silence he gave her time to form her thoughts. He wasn't going to rush her, despite his ardent need. His eyes adjusted further to the weak light and the outline of her body became visible. His fingers continued to run though the smooth, sweet smelling tresses. Her head leaned into his hand and he felt satin lips kiss the palm. Sharp teeth nipped at the tender flesh of the pad below his thumb.

His other hand joined the first. Pulling her face close with both hands, he kissed her quickly then scooped her willing body into his arms, mouth invading hers, taking every silky inch of the moistness.

She was so small in his arms. A tight goddess for him to fuck. This was going to be amazing. Lifting his mouth from hers he looked into her stunning brown eyes.

"Where to, ma'am?"

"I'm not sure I can think right now. You're going to have to pick the spot."

Giving her lips a peck he smiled, gazing into her eyes. "I like that I do this to you."

Glancing around the dark bar his brain wrapped around an idea. Would she let him? Only one way to find out.

Rick carefully moved around the tables, her compact form held tight in his arms. God, she felt small and breakable against his skin. A sweet succulent doll for him to play with and pleasure. Still, she wasn't a toy. The smell of flesh, sex and raw need filled his nostrils as she pressed against him, her arms clasped tight around his neck. Sleek muscle belied her seeming fragility. No, she wasn't a toy.

Reaching the bar, he placed her carefully on a stool. Her pretty dress was mismatched, off by one pearly snap all the way down. Fingering the first of the silver edged disks he popped it apart to reveal an inch of honey colored skin to his hungry eyes.

His finger traced a line between the parted fabric as he watched her face for a reaction. Her half-lidded gaze met his, the corner of her bottom lip caught in even white teeth as she nervously nibbled the soft skin there. He understood how she felt. The trembling in his hands was getting harder to control as he slowly popped open another snap to reveal her soft, pink-tipped breasts.

His fingers touched the hard pink nipples, then moved to cover her perfect breasts fully with his hands, gently kneading the firm flesh. She leaned back with a moan, offering him better access to her body. He framed one sweet pert nipple between his thumb and forefinger, then dipped forward to suck the ripe flesh into his mouth. She was warm thick sunshine after a long cold winter. The hard nub in his mouth pressed into him, demanding more. He bit down experimentally.

Her hands fisted in his long hair to pull his mouth tighter against the smooth feel of her. He pulled back, letting her breast pop out of his mouth with a slurp.

"You like that, Becky, when I bite your breast like that?"

Her whimpered response was answer enough. With a moan she pulled his head toward her breast once again.

Chuckling, he obliged her, this time moving to the other breast. He could lick her all day, tasting the sugary goodness of her breasts, letting the feel of them fill his mouth, tease his groin. Obviously, she had other plans. Her curvy legs wrapped around his thighs, demanding attention to all of her body. Pantyless, her hips ground against him, her wet pussy needy as it moved against his fabric-clad crotch. His cock jerked, crying to be released from the cloth prison.

His hands ripped the snaps apart, pulling the red gingham fabric from her body in a smooth stroke to drop it to the floor beneath them. Ass on the barstool, she'd tilted back until her upper body draped over the bar behind her. Arched, she offered herself to all his naughty thoughts, and where Becky was concerned, his thoughts were very naughty. She'd laid out her tight little body to his hands, lips and eyes, the ultimate gift. She couldn't be more of a cute little present if she'd been wrapped in a red bow.

What should he do to her first?

Running his hand up the outside of her smooth thighs, he bent from the waist so his mouth hovered over her bare pussy. He breathed in the musky scent that surrounded her, bringing his raging need to the point of desperation. His tongue slipped out to connect with her slick folds. She gasped above him, so softly he felt more than heard her reaction as her legs tightened around him, pulling him to her. Her feet ran up and down his flanks, giving him all the encouragement he needed. Greedily, he lapped at her juices.

He laved from the bottom of her slit to the petite bundle of nerves at the top. She rewarded each thrust of his face into her pussy with whimpered moans. Little sobs of delight erupted from the depths of her, falling around them as they moved together in the darkened bar.

Her fingers twined harder in his hair, pulling him deeper into her. Mouth busy, he reached for the waist on his sweats. An impatient push sent them down his legs, but not before he reached into a pocket to pull a condom from its depths.

Sometimes wishful thinking is a beautiful thing.

Not moving his mouth from her tortured clit, he kicked the material off to one side. He straightened, drawing a covetous groan from Becky. His hands traveled to her firm ass and lifted it off the barstool. Their eyes met, mere inches from one another.

"I want you, Becky. I want to fuck your hot pussy till you're screaming my name. Will you give yourself to me?"

Fingers still buried in his hair, she dragged his mouth to hers. Her lips opened and the invasion of her tongue and the press of her breasts against him nearly drove him mad. He had his answer.

With her body laid out like a pagan sacrifice before him, he had to fight to maintain his control. He needed to pull it together or he would be about as impressive as an anxious eighteen-year-old boy. Ripping open the condom wrapper, he then unrolled it over his rock hard cock, his hand applying strong strokes to the already turgid flesh. Staring lustfully at his cock, she licked her lips in need.

"Wow, that's impressive." She gasped out.

Chuckling, he placed a hand on each of her lush hips and pressed the tip against her moist slit. "I suppose I should say 'thanks', but I get the feeling you're blowing sunshine up my ass."

Her mouth opened as he pressed against her. He felt the resistance of her cleft against the tip of his engorged penis. She gasped and spread her legs further, re-wrapping them around his body, hauling him against her with needy force as she tried to pull him inside her.

"I never blow sunshine," she panted. "God I want you inside me, now. Take me, Rick, fuck me, please."

He grinned. "My pleasure."

With that, he sank his cock to the hilt in her warmth. Closing his eyes to enjoy the ride of pleasure she offered. Her tight box pulled him in, muscles squeezing his cock mercilessly. He loved the feel of being buried in the hot wetness. He would stay here forever, but the primal need to move within her grabbed him by the balls, forcing him to withdraw from her only to plunge back into her willing cunt.

Again and again he thrust in and out of her greedy heat, her answering thrusts hot and hard as his balls banged against her ass. Rick was in heaven. The fevered wash built in him, flowing over every sinew and fiber of his body, then centered on the nerve endings covering his penis. The sweet agony built with every stroke. It pulled him into a universe only occupied by their hip-locked bodies and her softly muttered groans of velvet indulgence.

Ramming into her with as much force as he dared, her thrusts answered his and ripped his orgasm from him. Balls tightening, stomach taut, he pumped into her, losing control as she thrashed in sexual need, the muscles of her tight box holding his cock in a savagely tender embrace.

She moaned against him as she wrapped her arms around his shoulders allowing her nails to run the length of his back. With the bar in her back he had more leverage to piston into her, all the better to feel her strong physical reaction. Bouncing against him, Becky's cries became guttural. She shook as she screamed his name and shattered in his arms.

Watching her face as she came against him drove Rick over the edge. With a savage cry he roared her name, mouth open, face to the sky. Shocks rocketed through his veins like liquid fire. His hips lost control as he pumped his release into her willing body.

Holding her to him he drifted on a cloud of delight. Delicious sensation swirled over him as he registered the space around him. Becky's softness pressed into his, and the soft sigh and the look of contented satisfaction on her precious face brought a smile to his lips. She was a tigress. Even now he felt the need for her was not sated. He didn't know if it ever would be.

Something dark and primal swirled around his heart. Instead of fear of being caught in an emotion filled web, there was only joy. His hands grabbed her ass, lifted her into the air, cock still impaled in her pussy. Rick spun them together, then sat on the barstool, her legs draped over his. Lifting her slightly, he gently pulled out of her despite her whimpered protests.

"Sorry, sweetheart, I have to. I wish I could stay buried inside you forever, but it's not safe, honey."

He felt her weak nod against him.

Chapter Sixteen

Becky rested against the strength of Rick's powerful body, her naked skin enveloped in his strong arms. Her sigh came from the depths of her, let out in a shaky breath. She felt wonderful, sexy, and replete. Her climax a study in self-indulgent gratification. It left her vulnerable, but strong and wholly feminine. Her hands roamed over the powerful muscles of Rick's back.

She felt safe. Not, "princess in a tower", safe. That wasn't her style. Rather, safe to feel. Powerful, strong, arousing. Like a well-worshiped woman. Rick was fast becoming her place to land when the world was hard and cold. Someone to share her battle with at the end of the day, take away the hurt, and girding her soul with the strength to face the demons in front of her.

She'd never understood her girlfriends' need for long term relationships before. Oh, she'd wanted one, thought she'd needed it, but until Rick, she didn't have a clue what they were really talking about. She'd gone into the desert searching for something she thought she was supposed to want and returned with something she needed. It was a scary, wholly frightening and wildly inviting array of emotions. Stores against the cold of life's winter.

Shit, she was getting poetic. Her brain had warped into a re-enactment of one of those mushy poetry classes from college. It was almost as if she was in love or something. She mentally scoffed, then stopped cold. Her body become deathly still as her mind raced over the past couple of weeks. She tried desperately to renounce her thoughts. No one fell in love this fast, *she* did not fall in love this fast. Clamping down on her emotions she forced the cold whispering truth from her thoughts, muzzling them. She needed to beat them back under control. She could not love this man, it was too soon.

Her ardent heart betrayed her. Mad lust aside, she'd conjured a man, called him to her with girlish fervor. The circle in the desert had been about her dreams for what she thought romantic love should be. Here, in his arms, the reality was far beyond anything she'd imagined.

Rick shifted beneath her and his hand caressed her hair. It felt so wonderful when he did that, so sexy and warm. "Are you cold, sweetheart?"

"A little," she admitted.

"Come on."

Setting her down gently, he took her hand in his and led her to the office. He motioned for her to enter first. She stuck her tongue out as she passed. The sharp sting on her bare bottom came as a thrilling shock.

"Hey, you!" She spun in a circle and one hand reached for her stinging butt while the other snaked out and smacked his powerful hind end in return.

"So, you wanna play?" His eyes held a dangerous seductive glint. Her pussy tightened with lust as she smiled daringly up at him.

He met her gaze with a fiendish glimmer. She was in for it. With a yip she took off to hide behind her office chair.

Laughing, he followed her. "When I get you, Becky Blake, you're gonna be so sorry."

"Oh yeah," she challenged, laughing too. "Just what do you think you're going to do?"

"Spank your naughty round behind until you beg for mercy, then fuck you senseless."

The laughter died on her lips. She sucked in hard to fill her suddenly airless lungs. She felt the wetness start between her legs at his delicious threat. Glancing the length of his hot muscular body, her gaze stopped on the massive erection he now sported.

Deep brown eyes followed her gaze. "Do you like my cock, Becky. Did it feel good inside you?"

Her tongue snaked out to lick her suddenly dry lips. She felt mesmerized, ensnared in the depths of his obvious need for her. Unable to answer him or to put into words what he wanted to hear. She licked her lips again in a wordless reply.

Without warning, his arm shot out, grabbed her, then held her in place as his big body moved around the chair, a panther stalking. He lifted her unresisting body, dropped into the chair and placed her face down across his lap.

"What are you doing?" It came out as a squeak. As she struggled to rise, his leg wrapped over hers and pinned her down on his lap. A hand expertly grabbed her arms and held them behind her back gently, but with firm intent.

A hand roamed over her ass in sexy circles, caressed each cheek suggestively. "Sweet angel, I told you. I'm going to spank that adorable ass of yours, then ride that hot pussy hard. You're going to be thinking of my cock pumping your tight cunt every time you sit down on your abused bottom tomorrow." He hesitated. "Becky?" It came out a hoarse moan.

"Yes?" She groaned, breathless.

"Do you want me to stop?"

"No."

She writhed against him. His sexy chuckle filled her ears, making her cream with need for him. A hand moved between her damp thighs, parting them firmly. A finger dipped to her needy opening and flicked over her engorged clit. Her body stilled as she curved her back to give him better access to the sensitive bundle of nerves. He released her hands to caress her ass once again.

A finger flicked over her clit as his other hand connected sharply with the sensitive flesh of her behind.

Whack.

The sound filled the closed confines of the office. A low moan tore from her throat as the mix of pleasure and pain washed over her from the stinging slap. It felt luscious, dirty and incredibly sexy to be at the mercy of his hands and mind. Helpless to do anything but feel. Pain washed over her to settle on her clit as it converted to raw need.

His voice was low, husky, and full of need. "Do you like that, sweet girl? Do you want another one?"

"Yes." It only came out as a whisper, shock had taken the air from her lungs. She'd never done anything like this before, never even fantasized about it. Something about Rick ate away at her fear, leaving her feeling clean and powerful.

His fingers dipped into her slit as she wiggled against him half begging for more, half begging for him to stop this enticing torture and fuck her. Again the hand came down causing stars to burst in her field of vision. Whimpers fell from her lips uncontrollably. The combination of the sharp smacks and the teasing of her most private place proved to be deliciously sensual. Mixed with his husky voice, the stinging smacks turned her on more desperately than she had ever been turned on before.

"That's it, pretty angel, ride my fingers while I abuse your beautiful ass."

Her hips lifted, offering him access to all of her. Thighs parted, knees on the couch, she silently presented herself for more of his sexy abuse. She bit her lip hard as his hand came down again, then once more. His fingers played with her clit, while he flogged her tender flesh over and over. Sometimes hard enough to make her gasp, sometimes gently. After each whack the tips of his fingers moved over her clit to mix the pain with delicious pleasure.

She felt her orgasm begin to overtake her, felt the pull of it, instant and alluring on the edge of her brain.

"Shit, Rick, you're going to make me come like this."

"That's it, baby, come against my fingers while I play with your sweet ass. God your ass looks so beautiful with my hand marks all over it."

She pressed her pussy into his hand as she came in a crashing ball of white hot energy. Screaming his name, her toes curled in from the hardest wettest orgasm she'd had in her life.

He didn't allow her to recover. Turning her over in one motion, his mouth came down on hers, then bit playfully at her neck and jaw line. "Touch my cock, Becky, feel how hard you make me."

Her orgasm still rippled over her body, coming in shuddering waves. "Rick, in my desk drawer, condoms, hurry. I want you inside me."

Reaching out in the small confines, he snagged the handle, pulled the drawer open, then ripped the box out of the drawer.

"Get on your hands and knees, I want you from behind."

The raw blind need in his voice spurred her. She lifted off his lap and quickly positioned herself on the gaudy couch, showing him her dripping cunt and reddened ass. Bottom in the air, she arched her back, making it easier for him to take her.

"Christ, Becky, you look amazing like that. I want to be gentle, baby, but I don't know if I can."

"Then just take me. Just slam your cock into my pussy and fuck me for your pleasure. Please your body with mine. Use me." It came out in a guttural groan, unlike anything she'd given voice to before.

She heard the indrawn hiss of his breath, felt him behind her, grasping her hips with his strong hands.

"Are you sure?"

"Just fuck me, Rick. Now!"

Feeling the tip of his hard penis against the opening of her slit she wondered if he *would* take her gently. She didn't want that. She needed it rough, hard, raw. Her question was answered as his cock slammed into her, all the way to the hilt, over and over again.

"Oh God, Oh ,yesss," ground from her lips.

He slammed into her fast, then slowly. She felt him fill every centimeter of her. Over and over again he assaulted her with his hard cock, his balls slapping against her slick, sore, swollen clit.

She met his rhythm, bucked her hips against his, hard and fast. Feeling the pressure building for an unbelievable third time, she reached her hand between her legs to her clit.

"Do it, sweetie, touch yourself while I fuck you. You're making me come."

He pounded her harder now, pressing her into the arm of the couch Unable to move against him anymore, she could only take what he gave her again and again. She felt his arms tense in pleasure as he gave one last thrust with his powerful cock.

Moaning in helpless erotic joy, she came as he cried out in a primitive war-cry above her, pumping his come into the barrier between their bodies, cock twitching deep inside of her.

His weight collapsed against her back and, with his mouth beside her ear, she could feel his grin. "Holy fucking shit, woman. That was, without a doubt, the best sex of my entire life."

Smiling contentedly, she wiggled against him. "Mine too, but I'm not going to be able to sit for a week. Do you often spank the women you fuck?"

She felt him move away from her. She peeked behind her as he sat down near her feet. Had she hurt him somehow? She'd meant for it to be light banter, but maybe she'd let a carefully guarded piece of herself out as she spoke. She would have to watch that in the future.

He pulled her, unresisting, into his lap. "Look at me." His fingers on her chin, he delicately tipped her face up to meet his gaze.

"To answer your question, no. I have never spanked a woman before. There's something about you, Becky. Something that makes me want to lose control, to take you in every position, every way I can think of. Something that makes me want to tie you down and torture all of you with toys and my tongue. I want to fuck you, sweetheart, every hole...and I mean every single hole in your tight body."

His hand roamed between her legs as he spoke, coming to rest meaningfully against her tight puckered anus.

Gulping air, she felt her eyes widen, becoming huge. That hard yummy cock fucking her up her ass was not something she'd ever considered, and yet here she was getting hot just thinking about it.

"Do I scare you, Becky?"

Slowly she shook her head. "No, you don't scare me. You make me want you."

His lips met hers in a tantalizingly slow caress full of promise of the pleasure to come.

Breaking the kiss, she contentedly snuggled her head into the groove between his head and shoulder. One strong arm wrapped around her and she sighed in contentment.

She was happy. Rick didn't make her feel that way, but somehow he completed her. In an almost imperceptible way this man felt like he was a part of her whole being. It felt good and right. He tenderly laid her down, then joined her on the narrow couch. Their bodies entwined, she felt herself drop into a cozy somnambulant world where nothing could hurt her.

Chapter Seventeen

Becky was happy. Over the moon, dance as you walk down the street and not care who saw you, happy. The last few days with Rick had been sublime. Fantastic sex every night and lazing around together during the day until it was time to go to work. Their time together had only been interrupted once by a business meeting as he'd tried to sell his program.

Too bad she'd been plagued by a gnawing feeling that she was somehow deceiving him. She'd managed to successfully bonk the emotion down with a mental fist every time it rose up, but the whispers were getting louder now.

They'd finally moved on from boinking in the club to boinking in her condo and, once, when he'd had that early meeting, at his apartment. She licked her lips at the memory of his awesome body in an expensive suit. Encased in the well fitting tropical-weight wool, his ass had looked one hundred percent hotter than in the tight jeans, and those were pretty damn incredible on him.

They were lying in her bed, being incredibly lethargic. She'd been thinking about getting up and heading out for a bike ride, but the pull of his lickable body undid all her good intentions. Which spot should she start on? Her yummy daydreams were interrupted by the buzzing of his cell phone. While he reached over her to the nightstand, she gave some serious consideration to starting in on him anyway, phone call or no. His deeply furrowed brow as he perused the small screen stopped her cold. Something wasn't right.

He pulled away from her. His warmth followed him, leaving her chill in the big bed. She watched him stand and leave the room to take the call. Her heart sank. Normally he accepted business calls without a thought, often playing with her body as he spoke. This call felt different. She had a strong urge to stick her fingers in her ears, bury herself beneath the blankets and wish today away.

That's mature. Get your ass up and deal with it.

Fine, she'd head to the shower.

The hot water rushed over her tired muscles, a healing balm to the stress inducing look on Rick's face. Stepping from the shower, she toweled off carefully. The fluffy warmth of the looped fuzz recharged her body, the perfect prescription for her fear. She grabbed the first pair of clean jeans and shirt she came across and headed into the kitchen, following the delicious smell of freshly brewed java.

At first she didn't register the scene that met her. Slumped at her kitchen table was Rick, naked, a defeated air surrounding him. The cell phone lay across the table as if he had pushed it there in frustration, but at whom? Becky? His caller? His head rested in his hands, his whole posture overwhelmed. Without thinking, she walked to his side and encircled his strong shoulders with her arms, caressing his back with her body.

He reached an arm behind him and pulled her around the chair and into his lap Soft platonic kisses dropped down on the top of her head and a hand absentmindedly ran over her hair. His posture, touch and caress seemed to sooth *her*, not the other way around as she had intended. His detached air seemed to refuse the comfort she offered him, worrying her all the more.

"Rick, is something wrong? Did something happen"? She tried to keep the now mind-numbing fear out of her voice, but heard it creep in despite her good intentions.

"No, sweetheart, just some old crap coming to visit again. I hate to ask this, but can I come in late tonight? I know it's Friday, but it's important."

Her heart felt like it was breaking and she didn't understand why. He said all the right words, however his tone was distant, almost cold.

"Um, sure. If you want. I can cover you. No big deal."

Liar.

"Thanks, sweetheart. I'm going to take off after my shower. I'll see you later tonight."

Kissing the top of her head once more, he then used his hips to gently nudge her off his lap. As he stared down at her for what seemed to be a very long time, something that looked like sadness crept over his features. He drew a deep breath, turned from her, and headed into the bedroom.

She wanted to follow him, demand to know what was wrong, but she was scared. What if he pushed her away again? Against judgment and reason, she loved this man. There was no fear now when she admitted that, just a deep wash of joy filling her heart. Now that love hung by a tenuous thread, teased her with alternating pain and bliss. Something was deeply wrong here and she didn't know how to make it better.

He headed out a little while later. Hair still wet from the shower, pulled back in a long ponytail, he was heart-breakingly handsome. His eyes sad, he gave her a brief hug, then turned and walked out the door without his usual kiss goodbye.

Chapter Eighteen

The three glasses, joined together by their ice cold handles, moved under the amber flow as one. Each one was deftly filled and topped neatly with a head of foam, then passed to the impatient waiter tapping his fingers on the edge of the bar. Becky's smile seemed futile as she faced his impatience. All the waiters were out of sorts tonight. Three bachelorette parties, two birthday parties and an otherwise full house had kept them jumping like kids playing dodge ball. Worse still, it was now almost midnight and still no sign of Rick. Becky tried to put it out of her mind, concentrate on the noise of the place, the flow, but it was no use. Her mind kept returning to Rick's face as she last saw it, contemplative and sad.

"Hey, Beckers, it's a zoo out there."

"Thanks, Mr. Obvious, for that scintillating news flash."

Muscles grinned down at her warmly. "You got it under control back here? Looks like you're one 'tender short."

She glared up at the big man as she reached into the cooler for the wine, then poured a glass for another in the long line of expectant waiters. "Yep, you got it under control out there?"

"Yep. Nothing I can't handle. You okay? You aren't your normal bubbly self today."

"Sure. Why, don't I look okay? Just 'cause my hair's falling out of its braid, there's beer down my shirtfront and probably mascara all under my eyes does not mean I'm not hunky dory."

"Yeah right. You can fool some of the people..."

"Don't make me squirt you with the soda dispenser, Muscles." She sighed. "I'm just a bit short of help right now, but we've been there before. I'll make it through."

The music swelled as one the strippers boogied onto the stage in a full business suit. The crowd roared their approval and dollar bills filled the air, held aloft by arms stretching to be noticed like a classroom of teacher's pets with the right math answer. The place was hopping. Where the hell was Rick? She craned her neck to see over the crowd of torqued up females.

"Let me guess, you're looking for someone in particular?" Muscles voice rose over the shouts of the nearby women.

"None of your damn business, Wayne."

"Ouch, you know not to call me that here. You're wounding me." The big man clutched the region of his heart with two meaty paws. Looking deeply offended, he turned away. Apparently his feelings were unscathed because his barking laugh floated behind him.

Dumbass.

She was in no mood and the big lug just had to push her buttons. Push and push again. Grumbling, she grabbed the ice bucket and headed toward the back room that housed the noisy machine. One of these days she was getting one of those things installed near the bar. The haul was not far, but the way was often barred by the many bodies of horny women and oiled up strippers, making it one hell of an obstacle course.

By the time she returned with the heavy load, shoulders weighted down, her eyes spotted the familiar long hair and hawk-like profile of Rick. She let out a breath. It tasted stale

153

from being held deep in the bottom of her lungs all day. So the man finally decided to show his face. 'Bout damn time. Who the hell did he think he was, leaving the guys to twist in the wind like that? She'd give him a piece of her mind if she wasn't so happy to see him. Her heart felt like it was about to burst right out of her chest it was beating so hard.

As she approached him, the weariness that carved his face became apparent. His shoulders were uncharacteristically slumped, his head bowed. Dumping the ice into the bin she glanced at his hands, which were tensed around the bottle of scotch he poured.

Moving close, she touched his arm, only to feel him pull back.

Ouch.

She tried to keep her voice casual, not let on how much the simple action wounded her.

"Hey, Rick. I was worried."

Cold brown eyes bored into hers challengingly. "I told you I was going to be late. I was late." He turned his back to her and headed down the bar, drink in his hand.

Trying to hide the hurt in her heart, she smiled cheerfully at a pretty blonde woman perched on a stool at the end of the bar. She was one of those women who was the polar opposite of Becky. Tall, blonde, impeccably coiffed and gorgeous with boobs the size of Cleveland. She just bet that the woman's legs went on forever. Her low cut dress was stunning and the expensive cut fit her body to perfection. Next to her, Becky felt short, messy and unfashionable.

"Can I get you something to drink?"

"Thanks, I'm dying for a vodka martini. Got any Grey Goose?"

Becky nodded in affirmation then headed to the back wall where she displayed the expensive alcohol. Dumping ice into the shaker, she looked for Rick out of the corner of her eye. Damn, she was obsessing. She'd never done anything like this with the other men she'd dated. Until Rick, men had always been something she could take or leave as long as she had her vibrator.

But you didn't love them.

No, she hadn't, she reflected, but love was not an excuse to become the man's personal stalker either. He'd made no declarations, spoken no vows of undying affection. Just given her the best two weeks of sex in her whole damn life. She was not naïve enough to think that men saw sex and love as part of the same package all the time. Rick probably separated what they did from his heart behind a gated fortress of solitude. Wasn't that how it worked in the male of the species?

"Here ya go, that's nine fifty." Becky owned the place, set the prices, yet even she winced when she rattled off the numbers. Spoken aloud, the price sounded too high for such a tiny drink. Only the visitors ordered this stuff. Most of the locals wanted bang for their buck and stuck with the well.

"Oh, Rick said to put it on his tab."

The stabbing little pain Becky felt in the region of her heart wasn't easy to ignore, but she managed to cover it with a smile.

"Okay, sure. I didn't know he had a guest this evening."

The blonde leaned in conspiratorially. "Well I'm not really a guest. I'm his wife."

ಐ ಜ

Shit, the drama queen was talking to Becky. Even though he was swamped, he had to get over there before Tara said something stupid.

Uh oh, too late.

The wounded look that crossed Becky's sweet features told him that his ex was up to her usual fun and games. How she'd zeroed in so fast on the one woman in the world he wanted to protect from her was beyond him. It had taken what? All of ten minutes or so. He'd thought he could ignore Becky. That by not talking to her it would somehow protect the pretty, petite bar owner from his ex-wife's nasty claws. Tara had always had the bad habit of unsheathing them if she thought someone was poaching on her territory. While they'd been married, she had single-handedly ended three lifelong friendships he had cherished. Not cherished enough, though, he amended.

Pushing past the other bartenders, he determinedly made his way toward the pair.

It had taken Tara no time at all to come to the reason for her foray into what he now thought of as his territory. She'd run down the escalator at the airport, jumped into his arms and tried to kiss him on the mouth. Setting her down, he'd crossed his arms over his chest to dissuade further public displays of her affection.

Apparently all her efforts to get a job had stalled. She'd spent the additional rent money he'd sent her on God knows what and now she had no place to live. Tears had pearled down her perfect face. A face that, surprisingly, no longer moved him.

He'd seen this song and dance before. How could he have ever convinced himself he loved this self-centered woman? She was a dark cavern to Becky's warm golden rays. Just as soon as he called and spoke to Tara's folks, he was putting her sorry ass on a plane to Salt Lake City. Let them sort it out. Rick wanted no part of her three ring circus anymore.

ℰℭ ℭℬ

"I'm sorry, I didn't hear you properly, are you saying Rick's married?"

The other woman laughed and the sound reminded Becky of a description of a fairy princess's laugh she'd read about once, "silver tinkling rain".

"Well not technically, I'm his ex, but we're seeing each other again and it's going really well. Just as soon as he sells his software program I think he'll be joining me back in San Francisco."

Becky fought to keep her smile pleasant. She'd been going for cheery. No way in hell she could manage that now. "Oh, Rick didn't tell me that."

The woman smiled indulgently. "Well it's a fairly new development, though not much of a surprise. We've been talking ever since the divorce. It was only a matter of time before the resentments got put aside and we were together again. So, you work with Rick."

Becky nodded slowly.

The woman wrinkled her nose. "I can't imagine someone desperate enough to come to a place like this, but I bet the owner's super rich. Rick never talks about her much. It's nice that you can work in a place like this. I'm sure it beats stripping yourself, huh?" She took a sip of her drink then smiled broadly, her brilliant white teeth reminding Becky of a shark about to take a chomp out of a helpless swimmer in one of those adventure movies. "Hey, honey. We were just talking about you.

This woman was about to dish some dirt on the pervert that owns this place. I was going to find out if she screws all the guys as part of their audition."

Looking back, Becky saw Rick visibly wince.

"Tara, I'd like you to meet Becky Blake, the owner of the Buckin' Bronco All Male Review. Becky, this is Tara, my ex." Rick's eyes were mere slits, irritation showing in his every gesture.

"We've met, sort of." Crossing her arms across her chest, Becky hugged herself tight in the suddenly chill space.

Tara graced them with her tinkling laugh once more. "Oops, my bad. So, Becky, do you screw all the strippers? Inquiring minds want to know."

Her heart dropped within her chest. She looked up to see if anyone else heard the thunk of it hitting the floor. Other than Rick's assessing eyes and Tara's curious ones, no one else seemed to be paying attention to their little triumvirate.

"No, I only screw the people I think care about me, but apparently I've made a few mistakes in that area. You know what? Rick, you lock up tonight. I'm heading home. It's been a hell of a bad day."

Patting her pockets to make sure she had her keys, she headed to the front door, her head down to hide the tears gathering in her eyes. She was hoping Rick would stop her, but he didn't and that made her feel more like a pathetic fool than she already did. If that was possible. Looking back as she approached the door, she saw him still rooted to the same spot, staring at her with tortured eyes. Tears slipped down Becky's cheeks as she headed to the safety of her home to lick her wounds.

Chapter Nineteen

"Was it something I said?" Rick wasn't fooled one bit by the innocent look in Tara's eyes. She'd zeroed in on Becky and attacked without mercy.

He was a heel for not chasing after Becky, but he couldn't leave the bar. *Liar*, his heart whispered. He tamped the voice down, trying to ignore it.

"Tara, finish your drink. I'll give you enough money to stay at a strip hotel tonight. I don't want to deal with you anymore."

She pouted and her bottom lip trembled. "But, Rick, I thought I was staying with you."

"Yeah, I was almost stupid enough to let you. Luckily, I got smart."

"Come on, Rick, you can't be upset at me for talking with your boss. It's not like this job means anything to you. You're not a bartender, you're a software engineer."

"Tara, unless and until I sell that program I'm a bartender. I like my job, I like the people, I like my boss...a lot...and until you stuck your damn nose in it, she liked me."

"Oh for crying out loud, Rick, it sounds like you're telling me you have a relationship with her. A strip club owner? What about us?" Her eyes were wounded. Huge and luminous, they didn't move him one bit.

He reached his hand to the back of his pony-tail and tugged. "There is no 'us', Tara. There hasn't been an 'us' since I caught you in bed with someone else. You're only here to get something out of me. In the morning I'm putting you're manipulative ass on a plane to Salt Lake City. You can explain it to your parents. I'm done with you."

The shocked look on her face would have made him laugh, however this was not funny. His ex wife *was* lost and vulnerable. *Yes, but she jacked you around and broke your heart.* Though he didn't want to hurt her, he needed to push any guilt he felt aside and move on with his life. Letting her rely on him like this was not helping her one bit.

"Rick, come on. Look what we meant to one another, all we have. You can't send me home. Daddy's furious with me." Her voice softened to a mere whisper and her eyes rounded to their full kittenish appeal. There it was sitting firmly on her delicate features. The manipulative look.

He fought the desire to roll his eyes. "That's not my problem anymore, Tara. You need to go. You've caused enough trouble to last me four lifetimes." He sighed. "I'm not trying to hurt you, but we need to break off the cycle of dependency we're both in. Can you understand that? We're not good for one another anymore, and my clomping attempts to help you aren't doing you any favors.

With her eyes not meeting his, she gave her blonde head a reluctant nod. "You're right, Rick."

He moved back a half step. "I don't think I quite heard you, Tara."

Her chin lifted and her teary gaze met his. "I said you're right, Rick. I've been too dependant on you. We need to stop communicating. Or rather I do."

He leaned forward. "You don't love me anymore, Tara. Why the dependency?"

She shook her head. "No, I haven't loved you for a long time. Maybe not even before we got married. It just seemed so, I don't know."

"Romantic?" he supplied.

Her eyes scrunched at the corners and her lips curved a bit. "Yeah, romantic. Running away in the middle of the night with my brave. Right out of a romance novel. Was I a complete fool?"

His shoulders hunched. "Well if you were, so was I. I have feelings for someone else, Tara, very strong feelings. I don't know what's going to happen, but... I just don't think we should speak anymore."

Her words came out in a tremulous ripple. "Maybe that's for the best. It's easy to be dependant on you. You're one of the good guys. For what it's worth, I'm sorry."

He signaled to Muscles. "Can you make sure my ex-wife gets to a nice hotel on the strip?

"Sure, Rick, I'd be more than happy to."

She looked up at him once more, her hands out, eyes pleading, "We were good together, right?" Her voice had risen in pitch and volume. Rick looked at the big man helplessly. Touching Tara's elbow, Muscles leaned in to whisper in her ear. Mutely, Tara nodded, then allowed him to direct her out of the bar by her elbow.

Rick ran a hand over the base of his ponytail and tugged it sharply in thought. Shit this was a mess. He had to contact Becky. Well maybe after he'd given her some time to cool off. *Liar.* Scratch that, *he* needed some time to figure out what to say to her. He owed her one long assed explanation.

ಬಿ ೮ಃ

Rick mopped the bar one last time then stood back to study the surface, looking for any infinitesimal bit of dirt to annihilate. Telling himself that he did it for the good of the business, he ignored the tiny voice that whispered he was trying to make up for what happened earlier this night to Becky.

"Look, ladies and gentlemen, there he is in all his glory, Idiotus Moronus-Sapien. Or stupid, stupid man."

"Very funny, Muscles. Did you get Tara to a hotel?"

"Yeah, she's safely tucked away for the night. I've got the information here." He tossed a hotel receipt on the bar.

Examining it, Rick frowned. "There aren't any charges listed here?"

The bouncer looked down at his shoes. "I've got friends in low places. We took care of it for you. I just don't like the way she hurt Becky."

"Yeah, about that, how long were you listening?"

Appearing to straighten the bar stools, the other man concentrated hard on the task. "Long enough. She told Becky you and her were getting back together."

"Shit, I should have known. Damn, now what?"

"I take it, by your reaction, your little come clean talk with your ex was on the up and up, then? 'Cause I don't really want to kill you."

"If you're asking if I am well and truly done with Tara, the answer is yes. Hell, Muscles, she only showed up here because she needs money. I shouldn't have brought her to the bar but..."

Muscles grinned. "But, you're like me, uh? A knight in tarnished armor. You think you can fix the world."

Rick turned and pulled the cash out of the register along with the tally sheet to count down the drawer. "I don't know, Muscles. I just couldn't let her twist in the wind. I guess it's not as easy to let go as I thought it would be, even if she did rip my guts out and dance on them"

"Do you still love her?" Muscles blue gaze bored into Rick's. The cerulean ovals speared him in place. He quickly shook his head. "No, I don't love her. I don't know if I ever did. It's not like..."

"Not like what you feel for Becky?" He finished for him.

Placing his elbows on the bar, Rick dropped his head into his hands. His palms pushed into his tightly closed eyes. "Shit, I fucked this up right royally, didn't I?"

"Look, I've known that girl for a lot of years now. She's got a real forgiving heart. Go to her and tell her how you feel. Tell the woman you love her."

His head jerked up as if he'd been hit in the jaw by the big bouncer. "Whoa, who said anything about... I don't..." His mind raced over the events of the last few weeks. Becky in his arms, his heart, his soul. Wonderingly he looked at the other man. "I do love her."

The smile that crossed Muscle's harsh features turned them almost angelic. The other man reached easily over the bar and clapped Rick on the back hard enough to nearly knock the wind out of him. "Congratulations, man. You love one hell of a woman. I couldn't be more proud. Now what the fuck are you going to do?"

Shaking his head, Rick once again picked up a stack of twentys and prepared to count them, turning each one so it faced the same direction. "I have no freaking clue."

Muscles chuckled. "This should be an interesting twenty four hours. He nodded, indicating the money. You want some help with that?"

Rick grunted an assent. They counted the rest of the cash in silence.

Chapter Twenty

Becky watched Vivian lift the thin rose-colored china cup to her sienna red lips to slowly and rather loudly slurp the green tea it contained

"Men lie."

With care, the older woman placed the cup down with a resigned sigh, her bright green, all-seeing eyes lighting on Becky. "They have indeed been known to tell certain...falsehood...when it comes to their male needs."

Becky snorted. "So you're saying men lie for pussy."

Vivian winced. "Well I'm not sure I would put it quite that way, but yes, men do lie for sex."

"So, and correct me if I'm wrong here, you're saying that a certain amount of prevarication is tolerable when pussy's on the line? I wish they'd covered that in my high school human relations class."

"No, I'm saying that many men lie for, 'pussy' as you put it. I am not saying all men do. I don't believe that to be the case." Lifting her cup to her lips, she appeared to hide a smile as she slurped loudly at her tea.

Becky sighed. She felt like nothing more than a salmon trying to swim upstream against the current of Vivian's beliefs. There were never any winners in an argument with Viv. Only the gore covered corpses of Becky's decapitated ideas.

Becky leaned in to better make her point, her hands punctuating the air with her words. "Okay let's say, for the sake of argument, that it's acceptable for a certain percentage of men to lie for sexual satisfaction. But not the man I love, Viv."

"Ahh, now we are down to it. Men can lie, but not *your* *man*. Tell me, how did Rick lie?"

Becky leaned back and folded her arms. "He didn't tell me about his ex."

"That's not lying, Beckers, that's not telling you about his ex. Is there any reason he should have told you about her?"

"Well, no," she said slowly. "I just think he might have mentioned she was about to visit to him. Us having a sexual relationship and all."

"What did he tell you about it when you asked him?"

Once again picking up the small fragile cup, Becky looked pointedly out the window.

"So by your actions you're saying you didn't confront the man about the blonde temptress he used to be married to."

Becky's eyes narrowed. "I don't remember telling you the color of her hair. How did you know?"

The older woman's vividly painted nails moved mysteriously through the air. "I'm psychic, I know things."

"Yes, you do seem to have some ability in that general direction."

She cackled softly. "Well, it lightens my heart to hear you finally admit it."

Becky held up her hand to silence the seer. "Wait, I'm not finished. "Your ability has never before run to the hair color of an ex-wife." She folded her arms once again.

Vivian laughed. "Guilty. Muscles called me this morning." The look that crossed her face registered a lot of emotions, guilt not being one of them.

Becky snorted. "Fraud."

The redhead just grinned back at her. "I use my listening skills along with my innate psychic ability."

"So, are you going to share the upshot of this fascinating tête-à-tête?

Red curls shook in the negative. "Nope, this is your life. I can help you, give you direction, but I won't fix it for you."

"You mean you won't wave your magic wand?"

"I ain't Glenda, you know." She chuckled.

"Nope, poofy pink is definitely not you." Their laughter mingled in the warm coziness of the shop's tea area.

Becky became serious. "What if Rick's not the man I conjured, Viv?"

"What makes you think he isn't?"

"I don't know, I guess I was expecting..."

"What? Some man to appear at your door with a pink bow around his dick? That can be arranged, for a fee."

Becky laughed. "No, nothing like that, but maybe a sign of some sort."

Viv's face sobered. "Becky, there are signs all around you. All you have to do is look and listen."

Becky thought of the feather still tucked safely in her purse.

"I guess. I just thought that someday my prince would come. Just like in the fairy tales. You know, 'and they lived happily ever after'. I even used to draw 'Becky plus' on sheets of paper with a line next to it. All my girlfriends would write in the name of the boy of the moment. They'd dot the paper with little hearts like girls do. I tried to make mine like theirs, but I never knew anyone whose name I wanted to put next to mine."

"Until now?" Her friend's soft words seemed to shimmer in the air around them.

"Until now," she agreed. She took a deep breath, gathering her nerve. "Seriously, Viv, I want to go back out in the desert and un-cast that spell."

A weathered hand covered hers. "I'm so sorry, Becky dear. I know you are upset about the way things are going, but you can't do that."

"Why the hell not?" She pulled her hand from beneath Vivian's as tears began to cloud her eyes. She was acting like a petulant child, but damn it, this whole situation was a mess.

"Because it doesn't work like that, dearie. Imagine a spell as dropped pebbles in a still pond. You drop your stone, or spell, and send the ripples out to bring your desires to you. What would happen if you put your hand into the pond to pull the pebble back out?"

She scrunched her nose in thought. "The ripples would be larger and there would be more of them."

Vivian sat back in her chair, a delighted smile on her face. "You have a gift for understanding this stuff, Becky. A lot of people never come to that conclusion. They create a spell, wait for it to work. When it doesn't they make another and another, putting out random energy until the intent is so muddied even they don't remember what they asked for in the first damn place."

"What if..." She bit her lip in frustration. How to word this to her friend when she didn't even want to think it? "What if my spell is keeping Rick and his ex-wife apart? What if I ruined it for them?"

The older woman's lips curved into a small smile. "I thought you didn't believe in my Juju?"

Tears gathered again in the corners of her eyes. She chased at them with a furious swipe of one hand. "I don't know what I believe anymore, Vivian. I just love him." A sob caught in her throat, helplessly, she lifted a hand to her friend in a silent appeal.

Vivian rose and came around the table to give her a motherly hug. "Honey, your confusion and fear show your heart. You didn't cast this spell to entrap any specific man, you cast to find the love of your life. I would not have encouraged you if I did not think your motives were pure. If Rick's heart was not free, he could not have heeded your call. The magic would not have worked on him. The two of you belong together, dearie. I've seen it. Rick plus Becky, and they loved happily ever after."

"It's just all messed up, Viv. It seemed so silly, so innocent, a couple of weeks ago. Like a grocery list for the man of my dreams. Now... Well, now I feel like I have really hurt him, messed up his life."

The seer smiled. "I thought he lied?"

Becky shook her head. "No, I'm mad, but if I step back, I can't think of one reason why he should have told me about his ex. This is my problem, not his. I need to just let him go. Can I release him, Viv? Just set him free?"

Vivian straightened, speaking to her with the authority Becky usually heard her reserve for her pupils. "I don't think you want that, dearie. Take a couple days. Think about it, then if it's still what you wish, I'll help you write something."

After placing the delicate china on the table before her, Becky rose to hug her friend. "Thanks. I love you a lot."

"Me too, Becky dear. Blessed be, my child." One ageless hand reached out and traced a symbol over Becky's forehead, leaving tingling in its wake. It wasn't often Becky felt the power her friend seemed to wield, not often she believed without question that this woman had a deep understanding of the universe. Right now, in this moment, she believed.

Chapter Twenty-One

Hot sun streamed over Becky, baking her back. The combination of searing heat and her sweaty effort removed conscious thought. Her brain, stripped bare of the stress of the night before, finally found peace as she peddled harder in a woefully pitiful attempt to catch up with Muscles. He was beating the living crap out of her today. His legs were pistoning machines as he pushed her mercilessly. Every turn of the pedals, every shift of her body as she maneuvered the bike, made her lungs ache in her chest, her thighs and calves burn with the effort.

Suck the air in, push down, pull up, move, push your cadence higher, move. Bent over the areobars on the front of the bike, she pushed hard as she slipped into a lower gear, her legs loosening as she prepared for the run. Today was their brick workout.

Bike plus run plus ick equals brick

Straightening, she prepared to take the turn onto the cul-de-sac that contained the big man's house. Damnit, the fucker was already in his driveway. Peddling harder she watched him hand his bike off to his waiting wife, kiss her quickly, then reach down for his running shoes.

Pulling into the drive right behind him she stood up on the pedals, tossed a leg over the bar and jumped off the bike. Muscle's wife, Lacey, reached for her equipment as well.

"He's got you beat today," the petite woman laughed out.

"Not for long," Becky countered as she kicked off her bike shoes to make the switch for the run. Running shoes on, she took off after Muscles as he rounded the corner and disappeared from sight.

Turning her legs over hard as she could, she began to eat relentlessly at the distance between them, imagining a fishing line that she slowly reeled in. Just when she could make out the logo on his shoes, Muscles increased his leg turnover, upping the speed. Gulping air, she sucked up the tortured screams from her lungs to stop this agony and pushed herself harder.

It was a glorious afternoon. Dry heat wafted up from the pavement in front of her transforming dry cement to a mirage of cool water. Sweat dripped into her eyes, stinging them with salt. Ahead of her, the big man began to falter slightly. Smelling blood in the water, Becky poured it on, passing him just before the U-turn they always made one and a half miles into the run.

"Bitch," he huffed out.

Laughing, she hit it hard, her shirt further soaking with sweat. Even the super heated desert air could not wick the dampness from her fast enough.

Once more she turned, making a left as she headed for his house. His kids jumped up and down in the front yard, cheering their dad on. They squealed, "Daddy run faster, you can beat her."

Grinning like a fool, she hazarded a glance over her shoulder. Cripes, the man was gaining on her. She pushed it harder, but her legs were beginning to feel exactly like a bowl of

Jell-O, wobbly and weak. She dug deep, pulling the strength from an invisible well within her. Placed there from years of hard training.

The slap, slap of Muscle's shoes against the pavement behind her spurred her on. She was almost there, could feel the victory sweet in her veins. She wasn't letting this one go. Just behind her he was kicking hard for the chalk line in his driveway that denoted their finish line.

"I'm gonna getcha."

Smiling, she felt the inexorable pull of her own kick move out of her, pulling her faster than she thought she could run towards the thin line of milky white on the heated pavement. With a victorious cry she crossed a hairsbreadth in front of her friend, her cheeks aching from the wide grin she sported.

His kids swarmed around her. Their congratulations filled the air with as much fervor as they had so recently cheered their losing parent on with. She loved Muscle's fickle darlings, all five of them.

"Con-grat-u-lations, Becky. For your prize you get to pick a kid and take him with you. Just don't take my favorite." Muscles smiled.

The chorus of, "Aw dad's" and laughter filled her to the brim with an unspeakable joy and need. Each of Muscle's boys believed he was their dad's favorite. Each boy was right.

"Come on, darling monsters," Lacey's sweet voice rang out through the late afternoon air. "I've got dinner on for you. Becky, you can take the downstairs shower." Muscle's wife always cooked dinner after their bricks. It made Sunday night one of the best nights of the week.

"Thanks. Just let me get my bag out of the car and rack my bike. I'll be right in. Oh, and, Muscles?"

"What?"

"Thanks for today. I think I needed it."

He smiled as he boosted one of his rug-rats high in the air. "Why, Becky Blake, I don't know what you're talking about. It was nothing more than a good old fashioned ass kicking."

"Yeah, Dad," the kid held aloft crowed. "She kicked your ass all right."

Laughter followed them into the house.

Shaking her head, Becky popped the trunk and reached for her tri bag. As she wrenched it free, the black bag bumped against the large paper grocery sack that held the candles from the circle she'd cast. The time since the spell had been so weird she'd forgotten all about it. Shouldering the heavy canvas, she lifted the mass of melted wax. May in southern Nevada could be brutal. Dry temps well into the eighties over the past couple of weeks meant the heat index in her trunk would have been scorching.

Peeking inside, she stared at the twisted mass of melted colors, all run together in a kaleidoscope of reds, greens, blues and yellows. Colors selected to correspond to the four directions. Even the directional candles, large pillars all, had melted into a mass of colorful confusion. Peeling back one side of the bag to see more of the swirls of crayon-like color, her hand stilled. There, in an air bubble by itself, rested the red candle that denoted south. The direction from which the coyote had entered the circle. The candle that represented the man she'd called, Rick.

Lifting it carefully, she turned it over time and again in disbelief. It was intact, flawless. A bit of singeing on the wick the only sign of use. It's color vibrant and gleaming, no part it was melted or even warm to the touch on this hot day.

After dragging the rest of the ruined mass to Muscle's garbage, she carefully placed the red pillar into her Tri Bag.

This was ridiculous. It was time to deal with this head on. Tell Rick the truth and let him go. If it was some sort of real magic, then she needed to put an end to it, now. She loved Rick, knew that feeling was real. But she was not going to manipulate a man by means magical or otherwise, especially not Rick. He was either going to love her for her alone, or not at all. She had no intention of spending the rest of her life with someone tied to her by supernatural bullshit. Even if it wasn't true, even if the entire thing was a coincidence, did she want to sit around when she was ninety and wonder if he had really loved her?

If growing old with someone was in the cards, there would be no deception, real or by conjuring. If Rick loved her, then it had to be a real love, something to hold close for a lifetime. If not? She would find a way to survive.

Alone and crying.

As the spell said, so mote it be.

Chapter Twenty-Two

"Chicken shit."

Startled brown eyes met his in the back wall mirror. The bar had been busy the last two nights, but not so busy that Becky had any real excuse to avoid Rick the way she'd been doing. Every time he thought she was cornered with no way out, she managed to slip through an unseen gap.

It had been days since he'd held her, loved her body. Raw sexual need filled him. At his side, Becky's cheeks pinked prettily and long lashes lowered to conceal her eyes and her thoughts from him. She turned from him, once again about to slip away when, at the last second, he snaked his arm out and caught her by her elbow.

"Gotcha. Becky, we have to talk."

"Let go of my arm," she whispered, still refusing to meet his eyes. "*We* don't have to do anything. *I* have to go make an introduction. Please?"

Her head turned and she looked in his direction, but not at him, not really. It was obvious she had every intention of never looking his way again. Tough. She was not getting out of this.

"If nothing else, I have to talk to you about work, Becky. We need to sit down and discuss it tonight. Please, I don't want to wait until close." He could hear the longing creep into his voice.

Shit, he felt vulnerable with her. It wasn't a feeling he was comfortable with, but maybe Becky was worth it.

He watched her shoulders lift as she took in a deep breath, then, releasing it slowly, they deflated like a slow leak in a balloon. She crossed her arms. "Okay, fine, when?"

"Right after this introduction. Would that be okay? The sooner the better."

Her head nodded once before she stalked off towards the stage. Unashamedly he watched her go. He was supposed to keep up a front of being available for the ladies, yet it didn't matter, not anymore. He wasn't available and soon it wouldn't matter, he'd only be a memory here.

The way she reached for the microphone, held it gently, but firmly in her slender fingers was enough to drive him wild. Her smiling lips neared the enlarged end, a painful reminder of the last time she'd blown him. His cock rose painfully inside his tight jeans. Shifting the bulge as discreetly as possible, he looked up. An older woman with a head of flame red hair teased into a wild beehive hairdo held a ten dollar bill out in his direction.

"What can I get for you, ma'am?"

Merry green eyes twinkled at him. "Well I would ask you for a piece of what's come between you and that jean zipper, however it looks like I'm not the only one with a significant other here."

He smiled. "Yep, you're right. You better keep that down, though, or I'll lose my job."

The woman's head cocked to one side. Shifting the bill to her other hand, she presented her bangle encrusted right one to shake. "Hi, I'm Vivian, the owner of the shop next door and you're the one and only Rick Frazier."

His hand reached for hers. He found her grip to be strong and assured. "Wow, so you *are* psychic." Grinning, he motioned to the bar. "What can I get you to drink?"

"A beer, draft please, and being psychic is nothing more than listening to the information you're given. Becky's my friend."

His face fell as he moved his hand over his heart. "So you're not psychic? I'm hurt."

"I didn't say that, Rick. I said it involves listening. I get my information from many sources, some of whom would turn all that gorgeous black hair of yours gray."

He frowned. "I don't believe in ghosts and spirits and things that go bump in the night."

"Let me guess, you think its all bullshit and I'm crazy."

He looked uncomfortably away as he handed her the requested beer. "Um, you could say that."

"Don't let me spook you, kid. I wasn't reading your mind. A lot of people think I'm nuttier than a five pound bag of filberts. You're just joining the club. You don't have to believe in things that go bump in the night, but they believe in you, Rick Frazier." Her laughter was exactly what he'd imagined it would be, close to a cackle, yet delightful at the same time.

"Is there anything else I can get you?" He was a little disconcerted, not only that, he caught Becky descending the steps from the stage out of the corner of his eye. It was time to beard the lion in its gaudy pink den.

"Nope, you look like a man with a plan."

He grinned. "That obvious?"

Taking a thoughtful sip of the foamy beverage, her startling moss colored eyes bored into his. The color could only be described as piercing. Nailing his body in place, they seemed to scan his intentions. "No, just a thought I wanted to share with you, Coyote Man."

Rick's heart seemed to stop, then bang against his chest. A dream floated seductively on the edge of his brain before flitting off. Almost a memory, but gone, filling him with disquiet. "What did you call me?"

Her eyes sharpened, all humor gone. "Coyote Man, you'd know what it means if you let your heart remember. Listen to her, listen to her heart, not merely her words." In a twinkling, she changed. The serious countenance was replaced by good humor and a jaw splitting smile. "Well I gotta head home, the old man is waiting for me. Nice talking to you, Coyote Man." Downing the last of the beer in one gulp, she then headed for the door.

There it was again, that name. The name he'd been hearing whispered in his dreams. Odd, the woman was odd. He stared after her as Becky joined him, her presence palpable.

"Was that Vivian?"

"Yeah."

"What did she want?"

"Oh, to talk to me." His voice felt like it was coming from far off, like he was underwater. Shaking his head, he glanced down at Becky's sweet elfin face. "You ready for that talk?"

"Sure, I guess."

"Gee, the enthusiasm in your tone is bringing goose bumps to my flesh."

For the first time since the mess of two nights ago, she smiled at him. The light in her eyes warmed him to his toes. Well, if he was being honest, it did more than that. His cock knocked once more against his zipper. He was so not going to miss these damn pants. Maybe he'd burn them.

He watched as she tapped another bartender on the shoulder to indicate he was to take over for a bit, then motion Rick ahead of her in the direction of the office. He didn't want to walk ahead of her. He wanted to follow the sexy sway of her ass in the low cut jeans she wore. That was not happening, rats.

Reaching the office, she closed the door behind her. That cut off the bar noise as effectively as sharp knife cut meat.

"Have a seat, Rick." She indicated the couch with a slim hand. Her shapely fanny connected with the office chair. Poised at the very edge of her seat, she reminded him of a bird prepared for flight. Good thing he was between her and the door.

He shook his head. "No thanks. I'd rather stand."

She shrugged her shoulders and began to twirl a lock of her hair around a fingertip. "What's up?"

"You've been avoiding me, Becky. Why?"

Her eyes wandered to the two-way mirror and she looked out into the bar, appearing to search for something. "Is that why you've brought me here? I don't want to talk about that. There's a crowd out there."

Kneeling before her chair, he placed his hands on either armrest and turned her to fully face him. "We have to talk about it. I woke up every day with you in my arms, then you were gone."

She raised haunted eyes to his. "You know why."

"About Tara, I can explain."

Looking down at her lap, her fingers twisted together as she took her lip between sharp white teeth to worry the softness. He wanted to move his thumb to her lip, ease the tension he saw on her face, love her. He didn't dare, though. After what he was about to tell her, he doubted they'd have a relationship anymore.

"Becky, something's happened. I need to tell you, but I'm not sure how."

℘ ℘

She held up her hand. "Me first, Rick, please." She couldn't wait any longer. The guilt over what she'd done was eating her alive. Right or wrong she loved him too much to keep manipulating him this way.

Warily, he nodded.

"If you love something set it free. If it comes back to you, it's yours, if it doesn't, hunt it down and kill it."

She stifled a giggle. The tension in the room, along with the fear of coming clean played havoc with her mood. She'd been on edge for days. How many ways could you hide from a man you really should talk to? Putting this off had not made it any easier. *Take a deep breath, close your eyes and tell him the only reason he fell into bed with you was because of a spell. Fess up and tell the man you've kept him from the woman he loves, Tara.*

She couldn't live like this anymore. There'd been no sleep for her in days, just fitful tossing and turning as she'd flipped what she had to say over and over in her mind. No matter how she phrased it, there was not a way to make it come out as anything but an illogical, disjointed mishmash of stupidity.

"Rick, can you sit, you're making me nervous and I have to be able to get this out before I turn into a chicken and run away."

She watched as he scooched back to edgily sit on the couch. His turn to be uncomfortable.

"I have no idea how to tell you this. It's all going to sound so incredibly dumb coming out of my mouth. I can't let it go, though. I've talked all about it with Vivian and she says that the magic has nothing to do with what happened between us, but I don't know anymore. I'm just so confused."

Apparently she had his attention, his almost black gaze bored into hers. He was silent, waiting. Best to get it out in one breath while she had the courage. Now or never. She took a deep breath, then stood and paced the room.

"It all started the night before we met. You remember it was a full moon, right?" He gave a reluctant nod. "Well I had this spell on paper, but it burned. I cast it anyway. I thought it was dumb, but my vibrator died and when I went to sleep there was this coyote and the next day I met you and you had the hair and that feather... So the only reason you wanted to be with me was the spell and now you're ex-wife's back and I'm keeping you two apart and I just can't do that, Rick." Gasping for breath she looked at his tight face. He didn't look angry as much as confused and a litte bit shocked.

"What did you say about a coyote?"

"I dreamed about him. He turned into a man, into you. Oh God, Rick, I am so, so sorry." Her head dropped to her hands. Tears threatened to spill over and make more of a fool of her. She felt like a world class dork.

He blinked. "I don't really understand what's going on here, Becky. Are you saying that you went into the desert and did something to bring the two of us together and that it's keeping me apart from Tara?" He sounded confused. A strong hand ran the length of his hair. "I don't get it and, to be honest with you, I'm not sure I want to. He shook his head. "Now I have something I need to tell you, Becky. It's important.

౭ఎ ⚬ఇ

What the heck was that all about? Spells? Coyotes changing? He couldn't wrap his brain around it. He had to tell her, now. He couldn't string her along like this.

Frightened eyes flew to his and searched his face. "Just say it, Rick."

"I sold my program."

He watched her face closely for a reaction. Her worried look morphed to joy before his eyes.

"Rick, that's fantastic, I am so happy for you! This is great news." She plopped down on the couch and hugged him tight.

"Well, it is and it isn't."

She pulled away. Pearly teeth worried her lower lip once more. "What's wrong?"

Taking both of her small hands in his large ones, he looked deep into the gold flecked beauty of her eyes. "I can't work all night and be in meetings all day, Becky. I have to give you my notice. I'm quitting the Buckin' Bronco."

This time the relieved look on her face was unmistakable. "I knew it was coming, Rick. You never lied to me. I can't say I'm happy to see you go, but we'll get by."

That was it? Was it so easy for her to just let him walk away? Anger welled up from deep inside his heart. Anger and something else that felt an awful lot like pain. He squashed it down, and stood to pad in a wary circle in the cramped space. "Okay, then I guess two weeks notice will be fine."

There was that confused look again. It creased her forehead, rumpling her smooth brow. Full lips sank to a thin line, hiding the plump ripeness from his irritated gaze. "Well I don't see any reason you need to keep working. You must have things you need to get done, revisions. This can be your last night. I'm okay with that."

She was "okay" with that? Happy to let whatever they had just die right here, right now?

His voice tightened almost to the point of cracking. "Sure, I'll go after tonight. That's not a problem at all." He was being ripped to pieces inside, but he'd never let her see that. If she could be so damn cool then he was more than happy to follow her lead.

Chapter Twenty-Three

Hot tears swam in her eyes as a blood red sun sank into shimmying waves of heat at the edge of the dusty desert. This time the placement of the candles into a perfect circle seemed easier. She marked out the nine foot diameter with a four and a half foot string held in place with a tent stake. The whole process felt almost trouble-free the second time around.

Her hands shook as they reached into the bag, removing one small candle at a time as she marked the boundaries of the sacred space. Moving clockwise around the circle, her brow wrinkled as she fought to remember all of the instructions from before. Should she be heading in the opposite direction since she was trying to undo the damned thing? She just didn't know.

Hysterical laughter bubbled up from deep within her. It threatened to mix with her tears and overflow the tight dam she'd placed over her heart in a flood of wild emotion. She was a piece of work. If possible, she felt like even more of a dumb shit than last time

Yeah, this time you're throwing away a perfectly good man. Hell, better than good, damn good.

If she could reach up and flick off that red devil she would. Setting the last candle in place, she surveyed her work. The space was now complete. She stepped over the candles and into the circle, squatting to place a pink cloth on the ground. Her altar, the satin again held all the elements she'd need to cast her spell of un-doing. As she smoothed the glossy fabric over the soft sandy texture of the ground, fat salty teardrops rained over the cloth. Each wet blob stained the surface in an uneven pattern, then dried almost instantly in the moistureless climate. A butter knife replaced Vivian's ritual blade, it would have to suffice. She'd snuck off without telling her friend what she planned to do. Casting this spell would let Vivian down. She never wanted to see hurt in her friends eyes.

Huh. It's not like she won't figure it out.

"Shut up already. Sheesh."

The circle complete, she only had to wait for full dark. There was no way she was staying till midnight this time, she'd been wigged out enough before. She'd just have to cast and hope that the Gods understood why one small woman would chicken out about staying in the desert till the middle of the night.

Courage is a fleeting thing when you're heart's on the line.

Stepping out of the space she picked up the last two wax pillars. Her walk measured and ceremonial, she placed the green candle with care into the now cooling sand to mark north. Pacing the outside of the circle one last time, she prepared to place the red pillar, the same one she'd found in her trunk.

Her fingers played over it. Caressing the smooth surface lovingly, she sank to her knees on the dry earth. How could she let this wonderful man go? Her heart felt broken into brittle little bits, too small to fit back together into a cohesive whole. Oh, life would go on. She'd work at the bar, be a success, maybe even meet someone she could love enough to raise children with someday, when she was ready. But love with the depth of emotion she felt for Rick? No. She was afraid this special feeling would elude her the rest of her life. Rick Frazier was it for Becky Blake. She'd love him forever and always.

What a sap.

She snorted. Yeah, she most certainly was a sap, but never again. After tonight she'd wrap her heart up so tight it would never escape. There would be no more all-encompassing love that took away her reason.

You could just pick all this stuff up, head home, and take him, magic and all. Who would ever know?

It was tempting, so tempting. Yes, it would be the coward's way out, but she'd be a coward in the arms of Rick Frazier instead of an honorable woman all alone.

Head back, she shouted to the now starry sky, "Tell me what to do!"

No answer came, none would come. There was no knight on a horse waiting beyond the cactus to save her. No prince to carry her off to his palace. No man with long black hair and a devilish smile to lift her to her feet and declare his undying love, the veil of magic ripped from his eyes, his love alive despite the deception. She squatted alone in the chill twilight.

With firm resolution she sank the candle hard into the ground with more force than she needed to. Circling, again from north to south, she began to light each wick in turn. Votives shimmered as she moved to the large directional pillars.

"North for woman, born of earth, full of love and full of mirth.

East for the air, wind and breath. The newness of beginnings, not of death.

South is man, straight and hot, burn the fires in the pot.

West of water and of blood, in my veins I feel thy flood.

I cast this circle roundabout, now I enter without doubt."

What a joke. She was full of doubt, full of fear. She stepped from her simple yellow sundress and unbound her hair. Naked, save for the silver locket and the white feather in her hand, she took a deep cleansing breath. Head high she walked into the circle.

Her body lay as before, her head pillowed on the stark bare ground. She felt the texture under and around her. The smell of clean dry gravel and sand enveloped her, took her out of herself and into the magic of this place. The out of body feeling made it easier to speak the words that felt carved in her heart. The words to free the man she loved.

"Born of earth, of the earth, death in earth. I call upon you..." *Screw it.* Hey, Aphrodite baby? Or anyone else listening out there. I ask that you release Rick..."

She sat straight up as her skin prickled all along the length of her body. What had caused the reaction? A sound? Head cocked, she listened closer. Holy shit, there it was again, a voice soft in the cool night. Her heart raced, fear causing her to swallow hard. She looked beyond the iridescence of the candlelight, fighting to make out the space the noise had come from. Nothing there but a tall cactus.

Oh my God, that's not a cactus.

A coyote howled as Becky sucked in air, preparing to scream.

Chapter Twenty-Four

"Vivian, do you know where Becky is? She didn't come into work."

The redhead gave him a long searching look. One jewelry encrusted arm gracefully lifted to indicate the chair across from hers. Lined fingers moved with purpose over colorful tarot cards. She was so relaxed and silent compared to his worried on edge state. Frustrated, Rick slumped into the comfortable wing chair.

One aged hand gestured eloquently towards him. "Maybe, maybe not. Is it important that you find her?"

Agitation turned his hands to fist. Mentally, he pushed the welling feeling back down, fighting to remain still. If he was going to find Becky and clean up this God awful mess, he had to retain what little control he still managed to hold onto.

"I made an idiot out of myself last night. I'm pretty sure I took some things the wrong way."

"Ahh, and now you can't find Becky. Now that you what? Wish to apologize?"

He ran a hand over his scalp. His hair was loose today, all the better to pull it out by the fistful. "Um, yeah, but I don't scc..."

She chuckled. "How that's any of my business?"

Defeated, he nodded.

She leaned in, her voice conspiratorial and husky. "Becky's my friend, Rick, that makes it my business to some extent. She conjured you into her heart and now she's out there in the desert casting a spell to let you go because she loves you too much to manipulate you."

That's it, this woman was certifiable. "Vivian, no offense, but what the hell are you talking about?"

She sighed and placed the cup in front of her with a soft thunk. "Didn't you listen to Becky last night, or didn't she tell you?"

"You mean that bullshit about a spell in the desert. Truthfully, I spaced it. The whole thing made no sense to me."

Her eyes glittered, almost like that of a cat stalking a wary rabbit. "Whether it's bullshit or not, Becky believes she pulled you to her with that spell, Rick, and if you love her like I think you do, you'll respect that belief."

He threw up his hands. He'd been ambushed by the old lady and he couldn't fault her logic. Even if the spell was utter crap, Becky's beliefs were all that mattered now. "Okay, I give up. You're right. Now, can you tell me where Becky is? Do you know?"

She cackled maniacally, pulling a hand drawn map on yellowed parchment from the table next to her. "I think this might help you, young man. The place Becky has gone to is well marked."

"Thanks, Vivian." Standing to go, paper in hand, he hesitated, then leaned down to kiss the strange old lady on one weathered the cheek. There was something about her he could not resist. "You're a dear. If I was a few years older..."

"If you were a few years older you'd have to beat up my George to get to me." Her pleased smile said she'd appreciated the heartfelt compliment.

At the door of the shop, his hand on the knob, he heard her once again.

"Oh by the way, Coyote Boy."

Turning with impatience, he looked at her wizened features as they split into a naughty grin.

"You cannot enter the circle with clothes on." Her cackling laugh followed him into the warm arid sunset.

ȣ ʚ

Headlights glimmered off something large on the side of the road. Sure enough, it was Becky's little convertible. After pulling right behind it, he stepped out to investigate. Great, no sign of her. Well what did he expect? According to Vivian she was sitting naked several hundred feet off the road in the desert. He felt his cock harden at the thought.

Down boy, let's find the girl, talk to her, tell her we love her and then fuck her brains out.

He could feel the disappointment in the neighborhood of his crotch. His cock shrank back down in quiet obedience. His head had won, this time.

He headed back to his car and pulled out the map, a bottle of water and his flashlight. According the parchment Becky was close by, which was good. He was not a big fan of things that crawled through the desert in the middle of the night.

Despite the stars filling the sky above around him, the night was pitch black. His booted feet paced over the earth in long strides, moving toward...what? Had Vivian sent him on a wild goose chase? No, in the distance he could barely make out a low curve of light. The desert air was a deceptress, distance muddied into the dark of the night. How far? A few hundred feet, maybe less. Clicking off his flashlight, he approached the luminous glow.

His movements were stealthy, like he'd learned as a boy from his friend's grandfather. Closer now, he could make out the circle of sparkling lights. Becky stood opposite from him, naked and proud. Her body gleamed in the soft glow. She lifted her arms into the air before her, head tilted back, rose tipped breasts thrust high. With care, she stepped over the candles' fire and into the bright radiance of the illuminated sphere.

Almost without conscious thought, he reached for his shirt and pulled it over his head. Hopping on one foot then the other, his boots followed, dropped carelessly to the ground. Lastly, his jeans and under shorts met the same fate, heaped on top of the messy pile.

Bending over, he placed the map down, carefully securing it with the weight of the flashlight.

He moved towards her, the siren's call of her body drawing him onward. Now she lay on the ground, legs spread. He could make out her sex, beckoning to him. Her voice rang out in the crystalline night air, filling the space around him. Gooseflesh tingled along his spine. Carelessly he moved closer...and his bare foot connected with a rock.

"Damn."

She sat up, fear filling her eyes as she stared wildly into the darkness. Seeming to hone in on his naked figure, she leaned forward, trying to make out his form. He saw her mouth open as if to scream just as a coyote howled behind him. The hairs on his neck stood to full attention. He didn't have time to acknowledge his own concerns. Her eyes looked round and scared. Time to calm her fears.

"Becky, it's me."

A small hand came to her frantically heaving chest. He ran to her, jumped over the candles and bent down to scoop her trembling body into his arms. The coyote howled again as her eyes turned wonderingly to his.

"You came." Reaching out she stroked his face, her hands like satin against the roughness of his unshaven face. Tracing his lips with her thumb, her eyes drank him in, disbelief etching their depths. "Are you real?"

He smiled. "I'm real, sweetheart." Hugging her tight he emphasized his words by dropping kisses over the soft skin of her face.

Tears traced down her cheeks and the emotion in her eyes robbed the breath from his lungs. This precious woman felt so right in his arms.

She looked up at him with a sheepish smile on her face. "I bet you're wondering what I'm doing here, huh?"

He nosed her soft hair, feeling its silk against the rougher skin of his cheek. "Actually, I was more interested in your luscious naked body, but yeah, I guess I'm curious."

He felt her hand whack ineffectually at his arm and he couldn't help chuckling. "I figured you'd tell me if you were ready to, sweetheart."

She sighed. "I'm letting you go, Rick."

He stopped the caress of her body, doing his best to listen as Vivian had advised. "What if I don't want you to, sweetheart? What if I want to stay?"

She twisted away, out of his arms. Kneeling on the ground before him, her hands fluttered nervously in front of her. "I'm not sure you have a choice, Rick. I cast a spell for a man. That's what I was trying to tell you the other night. I brought you to me. Tied you up with Vivian's...no, *my* magic. I can't lay any of this at her feet. Rick, I am so sorry. I didn't mean to come between you and Tara. I didn't know you then. You were just a dream..."

He gave her a hard, disbelieving look. "Becky, you mean to tell me what we have between us you attribute to this?" He gestured around them to the candles and paraphernalia. "You think that you somehow negatively affected my relationship with Tara? Honey, she and I have been over for a long time. I caught her in bed with my ex business partner. We aren't getting back together, ever. I can never trust her again."

She blinked, obviously confused. "You aren't? But she said..."

Sighing, he reached for her hand and twined their fingers together. "She says a lot of things, honey. She talks a good game, but no, there was never a chance between us. She was looking for money, sweetie. I sent her home to her father. He's happy to support her now that I'm out of her life. She wants security, not long lasting love. We had a long talk. She's not going to be bothering me again. I don't want her. I want you."

"Oh." Her mouth formed a perfect oval in the glow surrounding them, her eyes wide as she took in what he'd told her.

"Becky, what I feel for you isn't magic, it's real. I don't know if what you did out here brought us together or not. I'm not going to dismiss the possibility, but...I have a hard time believing in hocus pocus. I know my feelings for you are real, not pulled from me in spite of myself. Feel my heart, honey." He pressed her small to his chest as he willed her to feel the beating thrum within. In the darkness of the cool air it seemed to pound out of him, through his skin to the palm of her hand.

Her eyes rose to meet his, round wary, hopefulness filling their depths. "I don't understand, Rick, help me to understand."

"I love you, Becky Blake. I love your adventurous spirit, the strength of you, I love the way you give yourself to me when we make love. You're a dream, my dream. I want to build my life with you."

"So what are you saying? You want what, marriage and kids?"

He laughed. "Yes, I want marriage, kids all of it. A picket fence and a dog. I can't imagine growing old without a dog. But what do you want, Becky?" He held his breath.

She dropped her chin, appearing to study the ground as a smile curved the corner of her mouth. "Same as you, but with more sex."

He chuckled and pulled her against him. Don't worry, sweetheart, you'll get so much of that you'll get sick of it."

"Not possible. I love you too, Rick Frazier. I love you so much. I can't believe you really love me back."

"Baby, I'm going to spend the rest of my life proving it to you." He stood. "I'll be right back."

Her face scrunched adorably. "Where are you going?"

"To get condoms, they're in my pants, which are out there somewhere." He lifted an arm and waved it in the general direction of the large red candle that marked south. "Then I'm going to come back here and fuck you till you scream, beautiful woman."

Chapter Twenty-Five

She shivered in delight. The man loved her. Smiling thoughtfully, she rose and stepped from the circle. After the last trip she'd wised up and brought along a blanket. Cold was okay, freezing was not.

She felt radiant and full of joy as she spread the blanket down carefully in the center of the sphere of light.

Rick's solid form materialized in glowing bronze at the edge of the flames. The air filled with the lonely piercing cry of the coyote, and this time it was joined by an answering howl from the opposite direction.

She laughed. "Sounds like the big guy found himself a girlfriend."

His own smile met hers, his eyes holding an erotic gleam. "More than a girlfriend." Winding a hand into her hair and pulling her mouth to his, they kissed. It started gentle, almost sweet, his lips pecking hers, showering her in love and safety.

Heat built in her and desire tightened her pussy as she pressed her naked body to his skin, silk on satin, meeting in erotic desire. Without warning, his tongue invaded her mouth in white hot desire. The mood between them moved from easy and sweet to hot yearning need the moment their tongues clashed.

Hands stroked her back, then came to rest on her hips as he pulled her against his now erect cock. She'd never get tired of the thick promise of his flesh pressed into her softness.

Lightly tracing her nails down his back, she felt him shudder in her arms. Feeling bolder she moved them lower, exploring the firmness of his ass cheeks, pressing her hands against them, nestling his cock closer to her.

His hands moving to her cheeks, he pulled away slightly and gazed deeply into her eyes. The umber depths of his glowed with need. "I love you, baby. God, honey, I want you so bad."

No longer shy in his presence she boldly met his gaze. All pretense gone, just herself in its place. No games, no hiding, not anymore, not from herself and not from this man. "I love you too."

Her words were simple, without artifice. His mouth once again crushed hers, consuming her in the fire they created together.

Cupping her breast in his hand, his thumb stroked her nipple. "I love the way you respond to me, how hard your lickable tits get. Look at your breast, Becky. Watch me pleasure you. I want to do this to you for the rest of my life."

Her eyes drifted down to where his strong brown hand hovered over the pink-tipped white skin. Her nipple, hard and wanting, waited for his touch. Pinching it between his thumb and forefinger he twisted the sensitive flesh slightly, pulling a cry of pleasure from her throat.

His voice was husky with need, thick with want. "Do you like that, Becky, when I touch you roughly like that? Do you want it hard and deep, fucking without mercy, or soft and sweet. Tell me what you want, sweetheart."

It felt like her eyes had glazed over. She could see, but the cloud of desire his words evoked made it hard to focus.

Moaning in answer, she pressed her breast harder into his hand, willing him to touch her roughly, then lick away the mix of pleasure and pain with his long tongue.

He chuckled low in her ear. "I'm going to take that for a both, sweet angel."

Pushing her down to the ground, he loomed over her. His long hair curtained her face, blocking the star filled night from her vision. Her world became his beautiful desire-filled face.

Beginning to trace his mouth down the length of her body, he licked, bit and kissed his way to her breast. Sucking the hard nub into his mouth, she felt his sharp teeth bite her in a way almost beyond erotic enjoyment, stopping just short of her threshold. Her fingers twined in his hair, pressed his face to her, cradled it as he suckled her.

Licking a wet trail to her other breast, he laved attention on it as well. He was driving her wild. Her hips rose, pressed towards him, as he bit, once again, at the other inflamed bud.

Mewling sounds flowed from her lips. Searing heat focused between her legs as her pussy became slick and juicy in preparation for the assault to come from his thick hard-on.

"Oh God, Rick, fuck me."

His mouth moved lower, kissing down her belly, now pulled taut with desire. His lips hovered above her pussy and she felt his hot breath on her lips. Wildly she bucked her hips towards them in greedy need.

His low laughter filled her ears, teasing her, making her already damp places flood with cream. "You want me to fuck you, sweetheart? Where do you want it? Here?" His fingers traced the outline of the entrance to her slit.

Moaning in response, she tried to move to encourage him to slip them inside and slake her need.

"Or will you let me fuck you here? Will you trust me enough for this? I wonder…"

His fingers dipped lower, pressing on the soft puckered flesh of her anus. She'd rarely considered it before, always thinking of anal sex as somehow gross and unappealing, but here, under the blanket of stars, with the soft desert noises all around them, she felt her blood flame in acceptance.

His finger pressed insistently into her, the pressure steady, enticing. Finally his tongue moved against her, adding to the urgent push of his finger against her tight little asshole. Its rough texture moved between the folds of her body, parting her lips, teasing her clit.

For a heart stopping moment the lapping tongue halted. Feeling his head pull away from her she entwined her fingers deeper into his hair, pulling him back to the button hardness of her clit.

His low chuckle filled her ears once more. "Don't worry, sweetheart, you'll come soon, again and again."

She watched with desiring eyes as his hand reached to the silk altar which lay on the ground to her left. His strong fingers connected with the rose scented massage oil and he drew it back to him. Working some into his hands, his lips once more connected with her tender swollen flesh.

His fingers, now slick with oil, circled her asshole. The gentle insistent pressure opened her virgin hole to accept a thick digit.

Her hips drove her pussy against his mouth, tongue and teeth. It hurt, but not in the way she had feared it would. Pleasure rocketed through her as the sharp sting subsided. Relaxing against him, allowing him manipulate her body, she felt his finger press into her sensitive dark hole further.

"Do you like that? Do you want more?"

His breath against her clit made her shake to be completed. Sexy sounds rose from her throat.

"Tell me, Becky. Tell me what you want."

"All of it, anything you want to do to me. Anything. My body is your toy. Please..." This last moaned in need.

"Please what, sweet girl?"

"Please take me. Anything, fuck me, anywhere."

She heard him growl in triumph. Head thrown back, she stared up at the star filled night that seemed to press down on their naked bodies. A finger replaced his tongue against her clit. Barely stoking the nerve filled flesh, he pulled her higher into the maddening desire. Her orgasm built within her, then burst forth, washing over her body in spasming waves.

"That's it, baby, come for me."

Gasping, she rucked the blanket beneath them with her hands, twisting the fabric hard as her release pulsed over her. Again and again she shuddered, shaking against his hand. Hips rolling, she was almost unaware of the finger in her tight hole.

Before she could return to earth from the most intense orgasm of her life, he moved to loom above her. His legs parted her thighs.

"Look down, honey, watch me fill you with my cock."

Tearing her gaze from his, she looked between their bodies to the place where his condom covered cock toyed at the opening of her vagina. The pressure increased against her as, with one motion, he fucked her all the way to the hilt. He pulled his hips back until just the tip of this cock remained in her, then once again pumped into her. The sensation, on top of her orgasm, felt electric.

Each thrust, faster and harder than the one before, soon forced her to wrap her legs around him to hang on. Nails dug into his back, she became a voracious animal, bucking wildly against his hard body in the night.

Pounding more urgently into her soaked pussy, she felt him shake, knew he danced on the edge of his own orgasm. Clamping the muscles of her vagina down hard against his cock she made her passage as tight as possible to pleasure him.

"Shit, Oh, Becky. Oh that's so good. I'm going to lose control in you, sweetheart."

Wrapping her legs tighter in answer, her hips bumped hard against his with every thrust. She grabbed his ass cheeks, squeezed them hard. Encouraged the furious thrust of his body into hers.

Animal-like, he howled against her, pumped his cock in ecstasy and came.

His gorgeous thick cock twitched inside of her as he rose on the wings of his own orgasm. His sexy face filled with a delighted look.

Crashing against her body, a lazy smile crossed his lips. "God, you're heaven."

She laughed. "I have to say the same right back atcha stud."

A playful nip at her neck was soon soothed by his tongue drawing a lazy circle. "Honey, you ain't seen nothing yet. You're not going to get much sleep tonight."

"Umm, are you psychic?"

Pulling away he grinned down at her. "Nope, just one horny, in love, guy."

"Hmm," she said thoughtfully. "I have been seriously considering instituting a one orgasm per night limit to avoid getting bored by over stimulation."

"Okay, you can have one orgasm a night. As for me..." He gestured to the condoms.

Her eyes took in the pile for the first time. Her lids closed as helpless laughter filled her. "How many of those did you bring, stud-muffin?"

Grinning lasciviously, he replied, "Oh, you know, a guy can have hope."

His cock had sprung to attention between them once again.

"So, Miss Blake, you ready for round two."

"Lord have mercy."

⧉ ⧉

He ran a hand up and down her sexy thigh. "I'll take that as a 'yeah'?"

She shook her head and a sly little smile hovered on her lips. "That's a 'hell yeah' to you."

Laughing he nipped at her ear. "By the time this night's over, darling, you aren't going to be able to sit down for a week."

"Good." He felt her hips wiggle against his, arousing him even more. Already he was hard, ready to take her again. Normally he wouldn't think this possible, but this woman made him want things he never had before.

Her tongue licked his ear, sending shivers down to his toes and back up to his almost painfully swollen cock. Pressing his shoulder with a small hand, she rolled him over. Lying on his back, naked, with a billion burning points of cold light above him, he relaxed, enjoying her tongue as it moved south.

No one had ever sucked his cock like this woman. She did it unselfishly, seeming to relish her ability to pull the come out of him with her mouth alone. She always looked amazed and pleased when he lost control in her mouth and bucked against her helplessly.

Tingles charged over him as she licked at his stomach like a kitten lapping milk. She was innocent and seductress bundled into one sexy petite package. He couldn't get enough of her.

Her lips hovered over his cock, making it leap and twitch in eagerness to meet the soft silken mouth. Anticipation made him almost desperate to be inside her, but he fought it down. Forced himself to watch and wait for her touch.

It didn't take long for his desire to be fulfilled. Her tongue darted out to lick the swollen tip of his hard cock. Again and again it touched him, sending stars exploding through his body and dancing into his brain.

With a naughty grin, she plunged the length of him into her mouth almost to the hilt. Her nimble tongue caressed the back of his shaft while she licked it.

"Holy shit, Becky, you're terrific at that."

Popping the engorged member out of her mouth while stroking it with her hand, she grinned up at him. "So you're saying I suck like a Hoover?"

He gasped. "Nope, that's an insult, a Dyson."

She laughed then popped him back into her mouth with a wet slurp.

Enjoying the sensation of having his cock sucked so expertly, he looked up at the sky in horny happiness. As she pulled harder, moving her mouth up and down the length of him, his perusal of the stars refocused to the woman between his legs capably blowing him.

Feeling the pressure mount inside him he bucked against her mouth. A soft hand moved to the base of his cock, squeezing with surprising force as her mouth slowed over him.

"Not yet. I believe there were certain promises made regarding my tight virgin ass..."

His breath sucked in with force as he felt his cock almost explode against her. "Shit, Becky, are you serious?"

Her smile was seductive, full of hot want as she stroked his hard cock twice. "Yes. I'm scared, but I know you won't hurt me." Her eyes gleamed wickedly. "Not more than I ask for anyway."

"Oh shit, sweetheart—"

His voice was cut off as once more her mouth imprisoned his cock.

Seconds later she pulled off him and sat up with a seductive purr. With a flip of her body she curled to her hands and knees before him. She glanced playfully over her shoulder. "Is this what you want, big boy, to fuck me here?"

Her hand came down hard on her ass, her fingers moving over the soft globe, coming to rest on the tight hole.

Swallowing thickly, he could only nod like a hungry boy being offered the candy of his dreams.

Motioning her head towards the oil, she offered him a saucy half smile. "Then move along, Rick" Her tone filled with kittenish seduction. "My virgin ass needs a good fucking."

His hands fumbled as he placed another condom on his rock hard member and coated the thick shaft with oil.

"Rick, is it going to hurt?" The shy, scared little sound of her voice turned him on even more than the naughty girl that had encouraged him only a moment ago. His hands roamed over her back in reassurance, "Yes, but not for long, sweetheart. If you want me to stop, you just say so. I'll let you guide me."

Nodding, she presented her gorgeous ripe ass for his lust-filled eyes to feast on.

He moved behind her, hands stroking her beautiful full bottom. Reaching for the oil he poured more into his hand, running it over the crack of her ass and onto the tight hole of her bottom. His other hand ran over her slit and he pushed two fingers in and out of her wet pussy.

She hesitated, still for a moment. Then, with a tentative wiggle of her ass, she moved against the press of his fingers, pumping them in and out of her pussy, circling her hips around them. The soft light glistened off the sheen of the oil along her crack.

Covering his now throbbing cock with oil once more, he grabbed her hips to still the movements of her body. Looking down, he pushed the tip against the tight pucker. He almost stopped. The thick shaft dwarfed the tiny bud. He did not want to hurt her. Her insistent moans returned his attention to this the sexy goddess who'd offered herself so willingly at the altar of his body.

Holding the shaft in one hand, her hip in the other, he slowly pressed his member into the resistant flesh. After an initial hesitation, the head of his cock popped past her tight barrier. Squeezed close in the confines of the narrow channel, he wanted to sink himself deep into her flesh. It took all his will to resist as he waited for her to relax and become able to accept another inch of his rigid erection.

"Put your finger on your clit, baby. Touch that beautiful pussy while I fuck your hot ass."

She moaned and he felt her weight shift under him as her hand moved to her clit.

"How does that feel, baby. Do you want more?"

Her savage, "yes" caused more blood to flow to his already rock-hard cock. He slid forward a scant inch, allowing her a moment to adjust to his size before he pulled back. Then, carefully and with almost creeping slow movement, he pressed into her once again.

Her head angled back, a slim finger still on her pretty clit. He wished she could watch him take him up the ass, wanted to see her reaction to the pounding she was about to get from his cock.

Sliding another inch into her, her ass wiggled against him while he looked on in amazement. Her movements almost felt like too much. "Shit, Becky, slow down, you're driving me crazy. I want to be gentle with you."

"Fuck gentle. Just take me, Rick. Now." Her voice came out a cross between a growl and a cry.

The need in her tone spurred him. With a groan, he sank his cock to the hilt in the tight channel. He felt her tense around him, hold him fast inside her. Gradually she loosened her muscles just enough to allow him to pull out of her, then he sank back into the welcome warmth of her body.

He felt it then, a slight movement of her hips, tentative and careful against his cock. Rocking against him with more insistence each time, she blatantly began to fuck his cock as it rode inside her ass.

Pumping exultantly, her body tensed around him, her fingers driving her to orgasm. Toes curled, balls tight to his body, he cried out her name into the crush of darkness that surrounded them and exploded in mind-numbing orgasm.

His arms wrapped tight around her body as he collapsed on top of her. His woman, his love. Once again she'd given so freely to him, without game playing or subterfuge. He didn't know if he'd ever get used to the loving sexual need she filled him with. He did know he'd never take this feeling, or this woman, for granted.

Pulling his cock from her, he removed the condom and placed it with the other to hike out with them when they woke. He wrapped the blanket around them both, pillowing her head on his arm as he drew her body to his with a contented sigh.

His hand smoothed through her hair and he kissed the top of her head, over and over. She pushed against him, snuggling closer to the warmth he offered in the chill dry air. Hearing *her* sigh of contentment, he smiled against her. She was one hell of a woman and she was all his.

ಬ ಛ

Happy. That described the feeling that welled in her heart perfectly. Happy and replete with sexual satisfaction. Who knew that anal sex could be so wonderful? *She* did now. She had full possession of the knowledge of amazing sex. She nestled against his strong body. His hand felt good as it caressed her scalp. In the distance the howl of the coyotes reminded her sleepy brain of what Vivian had once told her. Sex in a magic circle was binding, it brought out all the hidden emotions. Yes, they'd made magic tonight together in this softly lit space. Joined heads, hearts and minds. Two halves formed a glorious whole.

"I love you, Becky, forever."

She sighed, content. For the first time no worries from the outside crept in to mar her bliss. No desperate need to be the best filled her, spurred her to wake early and work late. All she needed to be was the best she could be. Stress would return. She knew that. She'd have her night hours at the bar and Rick would have meetings during the day. But they'd work it out, make each other a priority. This was too precious to let chance intervene. They had magic, and it was never good to take magic for granted.

Smiling, she let sleep take her weary mind into its embrace, her body and soul safe in Rick's strong arms.

Epilogue

The sun had just begun to sneak over the horizon when Rick's stomach rumbled, waking him from a sound sleep. Becky yawned in his arms. He smiled down at her as she peeked one sleepy eye at him.

"What time is it, Rick?"

"I don't know, my watch is in a pile of clothes over there somewhere." He motioned to indicate the general direction of south.

"Well, it's obviously time for breakfast. I'm starved. Wanna follow me to the Peppermill for Eggs Benedict?"

"You're speaking my language. I'm getting up, I swear, but before we go anywhere I need to find a cactus to water." He pointedly closed his eyes, drew her close and smelled her hair. Flowers in the desert.

"Well, may I suggest you hurry, Mr. Wide Awake? In another hour that sun's going to bake us." The practicality in her voice finally registered in his exhausted brain.

He nuzzled her neck with lazy kisses and licks. "You'd look cute with an apple in your mouth."

She whapped him playfully. "I mean it, up. I don't want to be roasted. Come to think of it baked, fried or fricasseed is out too. Her voice grew serious. "Is all this real? Between us, is it really happening?"

His hand tenderly caressed her cheek as he looked into her eyes. He bared all her emotion for her there, tried to convey his naked vulnerability. He felt her indrawn breath, the love on his face mirrored on her own. "Yes, it's real. Believe in me, Becky. Believe in the man, as well as the magic."

He watched her rise and gather her things. Tossing the sundress over her naked body, she reached inside her bag and after withdrawing her brush, she began to work on the tangles in her long hair.

Stretching, he too rose, finally heading for the nearest cactus.

He returned a minute later and began to search the area, making sure the desert was as clean as if they'd never been there.

"You know," she said casually. "I meant to ask you, but I keep forgetting. How did you find me last night?"

Picking up an errant candle that must have been knocked out of the way in the throes of their passion, he replied, "Vivian, she gave me a map that showed me where to find you."

Out of the corner of his eye he saw her freeze. Something in her stance alarmed him and shots of electricity zapped up and down his spine.

"A map? How is that possible? I never told her what I was going to do and the first time I only told her I was headed to 'the desert'."

Frowning, he headed to his pile of clothes. There, in a neatly folded pile much different than the way he'd left them the night before, sat his pants, underwear, shirt and boots with his socks tucked neatly inside. To one side lay his flashlight, alone. The hand-drawn parchment map was nowhere to be seen.

"It's gone. How the..." His eyes scanned the barren ground that surrounded the flashlight for any hint of the paper. There was no sign of it.

Pulling on his clothes, he reached down to pat his pockets for his keys. His hand brushed against something oddly shaped and unfamiliar wedged tight in the watch pocket. He didn't remember putting the map there, and for sure his pocket had been empty last night. Confused, he pulled the thing out. Folded parchment, just like the map.

He yelled out. "Hey I found it." He motioned for Becky to join him as he unfolded the paper and looked down. Nah, it couldn't be.

"Holy shit."

"What?" She came up beside him and her soft body leaned into his. She peeked around his shoulder.

He glanced up. Suspiciously, he surveyed the area around them, but no one was there. Years spent camping in the wilderness had honed his senses razor sharp. They would have alerted him if someone had tried to sneak up on them in the night, even someone as wily as Vivian. Head tilting to the sky, the laughter flowed freely. "Damnit, the old witch is magic."

Becky's brow cocked. "I thought you didn't believe in her hocus-pocus?"

He wrapped a loose arm around her shoulder. "Forget what I said before, sweetheart. I'm a bona-fide believer now."

He pulled her close and gave her a squeeze. Together they perused the words carefully lettered in pink ink. A lacy red heart surrounded the whole.

"Rick plus Becky, and they loved happily ever after."

About the Author

Nancy Liedel, writing as Nancy Lindquist, is the happily married mother of four boys (no, she is not going to try for a girl!). Two adopted and two made the old fashioned way.

Nancy never does anything by half measures. She adores travel, and her favorite trips are once yearly weekends in Las Vegas and as many cruises as she can talk her husband into. Her cruise history has included the listing event on Crown Princess in 2006. This did not stop her. She booked another cruise on the Crown the moment she got home! She's traveled to many other countries and has never had a travel experience she would not repeat.

As a writer of erotic romance, Nancy is always taking mental notes wherever she goes. Nancy loves life and attacks it with gusto, leaving her wonderful husband and number one inspiration, Gene, to follow along laughing and shaking his head in her wake.

A lover of romance since she was passed "Shana" under the table in tenth grade study hall by a friend of hers, Nancy finds the uninhibited world of Erotic Romance to be the perfect foil for her wit and naughty imagination.

Nancy loves e-mail from her readers. She blogs daily about life and travel on http://www.blog.liedel.org and writes about erotic romance at http://www.nancylindquist.com. You can send Nancy e-mail at nancy@liedel.org. She loves to hear from her readers.

Look for these titles

Lady Lillian's Guide to Amazing Sex

Printed in the United States
74467LV00002B/25-141

9 781599 984049